From the arcologies `P9-DBJ-873` Ring, uncover the . . .

MYSTERIES OF THE NIGHT'S DAWN UNIVERSE

- Why is the Kulu Intelligence Service so feared?

- What are the differences between blackhawks and voidhawks?

- Why can't the Weeping Rose be grown anywhere except on Norfolk?

- Why are Cosmoniks so modified, and are they all still human?

- What do Kiint really look like?

- Why is the Jiciro world off-limits?

- Why did the Nyvan colony collapse into war and anarchy?

- Why is life better in the Halo than on Earth?

The answers to these and many other questions are contained in a companion guide as wondrous and revealing as only the epic scope of The Night's Dawn could provide . . .

THE CONFEDERATION HANDBOOK

ACCLAIM FOR PETER HAMILTON'S TRILOGY
THE REALITY DYSFUNCTION
THE NEUTRONIUM ALCHEMIST
THE NAKED GOD

"This series is taking on one of sf's (and maybe all of literature's) primal jobs: the creation of a world with the scale and complexity of the real one." **—Locus**

more . . .

THE
CONFEDERATION
HANDBOOK

PETER F. HAMILTON

THE
CONFEDERATION
HANDBOOK

ASPECT®

WARNER BOOKS

An AOL Time Warner Company

WARNER BOOKS EDITION

Copyright © 2000 by Peter F. Hamilton
All rights reserved. No part of this book may be reproduced in any form or by any electronic or mechanical means, including information storage and retrieval systems, without permission in writing from the publisher, except by a reviewer who may quote brief passages in a review.

Cover design by Don Puckey
Cover illustration by Jim Burns
Digital Imaging by Shasti O'Leary

Aspect® name and logo are registered trademarks of Warner Books, Inc.

This Warner Books edition is published by arrangement with Macmillan Publishers Ltd, UK.

Warner Books, Inc., 1271 Avenue of the Americas, NY, NY 10020

Visit our Web site at www.twbookmark.com.

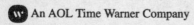 An AOL Time Warner Company

Printed in the United States of America

First Warner Books Printing: March 2002

10 9 8 7 6 5 4 3 2 1

ATTENTION: SCHOOLS AND CORPORATIONS
WARNER books are available at quantity discounts with bulk purchase for educational, business, or sales promotional use. For information, please write to: SPECIAL SALES DEPARTMENT, WARNER BOOKS, 1271 AVENUE OF THE AMERICAS, NEW YORK, N.Y. 10020

CONTENTS

THE
CONFEDERATION
HANDBOOK

THE CONFEDERATION
IN 2611

There are two major human cultures at this time:
the Adamist and the Edenist.

They are split by their different attitudes towards
the affinity gene.

One

Adamist Culture

Adamists define themselves as normal humans, a classification governed by their lack of an affinity gene. The name derives from the biblical Adam, who was first and therefore untainted. It was also an obvious choice, given that those who possessed an affinity gene were principally living in the habitat Eden at the time (2090) when the two cultures began to diverge (*A Second Chance at Eden*). In general, Adamists live on colonized terracompatible planets and in asteroid settlements. A small number live in the five independent (non-Edenist) bitek habitats.

Thanks to genetic engineering (geneering), average Adamist life expectancy is approximately 115 years, though this can vary wildly. Most Adamists are now the recipients of geneering performed between 2050 and 2200, with descendants of European, North American, and Pacific Rim nations benefiting from the highest level of enhancements. There are three Confederation planets which are settled entirely by humans who have no genetic manipulation in their ancestry, all of which have pastoral- or religious-based constitutions. Some enclaves of "pure" humans also live on other worlds, though their numbers are now in decline due to constant contact with their geneered cousins. Most of those groups were founded on religious or ethical grounds. Although isolated during the first stages of colonization, such separatism from a planet's mainstream culture is difficult to maintain. After learning of the outside world, the children of such groups normally find it very hard to understand why their ancestors have denied them this beneficial genetic heritage, and they tend to drift away from their enclaves.

With most hereditary diseases eradicated, organ efficiency improved, and substantial enhancement to the immune system, there is little need for geneering to be performed on fetuses now. The type of geneering which is still researched and practiced is concentrated principally on extending life expectancy. Among the very rich there is a fashion for having cosmetic geneering performed on their children; not just for classical beauty, but for blending of distinct racial traits, e.g. combining red hair with black skin.

The main exception to this slowdown of basic physiological alteration is the Royal Saldana family, whose members are still being modified for increased intelligence and memory capacity, and reduced sleep requirement, as well as expanding their life expectancy, which currently stands at 180 years. In short they are (ironically) becoming close to the Edenist ideal, lacking only affinity.

The second exception is the starship owner-operator families (such as the Calverts), who undergo dominant-gene modifications to cope with the long periods of zero-gee on their ships (again similar to that of Edenists). These families have eliminated vertiginous disorientation and organ decay, while bone-calcium levels will not decrease in the absence of gravity. Internal membranes are strengthened to cope with periods of high-gee acceleration (a function which is more commonly augmented with nanonic membranes), thus preventing organs from tearing, and their heart capacity has been increased to ensure their blood supply remains regular under acceleration.

Adamists, however, remain totally opposed to using the affinity bond (see below for exceptions). Although it began as a mild disagreement between users and non-users to start with (2050–2090), this attitude is now irrevocably entrenched among them, and has become the symbolic difference between the two principal human cultures. Because of its association with bitek (which it was originally designed to control), this affinity-bond technology has also been virtually abandoned by Adamists. Both Islam and the Christian Unity Church have proscribed the affinity gene as inhuman. The rationale is that the affinity gene is not part of the genetic heritage which was given to us by God, but instead was artificially designed and has to be sequenced into a fetus's DNA.

Geneering, which is the alteration (the more devout

say "tampering with") of existing genes, is permissible (principally because it brought so many medical benefits to the masses that it became impossible for non-fundamentalist Churches to oppose it). Shinto, Buddhism, and Hinduism are not so vigorous in their condemnation; affinity-bond domination of animals, or human communion, is not forbidden but it is frowned upon. No priests in those religions possess affinity bonds.

There are nevertheless some exceptions to this prohibition of employing the affinity bond. Because of cheapness, there is still a limited use of affinity-bonded animals on colony worlds in the first stages of their development (though never on Kulu Principality worlds), before an economy capable of producing domestic consumer mechanoids and cybernetics can be established. The application tends to die out after this phase, as servitor animals are replaced by mechanoids for all mundane tasks.

Such animals are mainly bought from Edenists, along with bitek products (typically landcoral for cheap housing). There are few Adamist sources for these products. Tropicana is virtually the only Adamist world which has no proscription against bitek, and its economy is based around selling affinity-bonded servitors and simple bitek to Adamists (it also has a large proportion of clinics offering rejuvenation treatments of dubious value). Bitek can also be purchased from the five independent habitats, which provide the most prominent exception to the Adamist refusal to use affinity bonds and bitek. These habitats are the main source of blackhawks, whose captain-owners are not the kind of people renowned for their religious principles. (For the origin of blackhawks see Valisk, page 208.)

The other exception of note is the Lord of Ruin, who is affinity capable (see Tranquillity and Kulu Kingdom, pages 127 and 108).

Nanonics

Nanonic technology is widespread in Adamist culture. It is a broad-ranging term covering both artificial neural circuits and cellular-replacement systems, as well as medical packages. The most common are as follows.

Neural nanonics, a web of neural-amplification circuits that are meshed directly with the brain, providing a datavise link with electronic circuitry. Most Confederation processors have a datavise facility, enabling an operator to interface directly with equipment, spacesuits, vehicles, etc.; this also provides a link with local communication nets. Other principal functions include neuroiconic displays, imprinting data directly into the brain; enhanced memory capacity; control over implants; and physiological and medical monitoring. Neural nanonics also receive entertainment shows in the form of sensevises, and can play sensenviron memories immersing the recipient in a total artificial environment that has video, audio, tactile and olfactory components, allowing complete immersion in fantasy worlds. The most popular flek recordings are mood fantasy albums produced by artists such as Jezzibella, which can also be used through direct optical interfaces, although these lack the full impact of a direct sensevise. Inevitably there is always a big market for bluesense fleks everywhere in the Confederation.

This technology is extremely prevalent, with something like 75–80 percent of Confederation Adamist adults on developed planets fitted with neural nanonics. They are implanted only when the brain has stopped growing, i.e. at sixteen to eighteen years old. For anyone involved in up-to-date aspects of modern society they are essential: fewer and fewer technological systems are being built with manual interfaces, and professions such as medicine or starship crewing cannot be conducted without them.

The distaff side of neural nanonics is sequestration nanonics, which can be used to infiltrate a person's cortex and puppet the entire body. These systems are highly illegal, and on most worlds their possession or use entails high penalties.

Government Intelligence agencies and the police forces of more authoritarian planets also use debrief nanonics, which can probe the brain's memory centers, extracting information directly.

Edenists do not use neural nanonics.

Medical nanonics come in packages of varying sophistication, which can be used for anything from patching up wounds in the field to complex deep-penetration operations. They consist of microfilaments with various functions, capable of treating individual cells. These include adding or extracting chemicals and proteins, filtering blood, knitting cells together (along a wound), and destroying and withdrawing malignant growths. Whereas first-aid packages can be operated by almost anyone with access to a controlling processor, the more complicated uses have to be supervised by qualified medical personnel. Medical packages are not autonomous.

Cosmoniks

These are industrial asteroid personnel whose bodies have atrophied due to extensive periods spent in zero-gee ("Astrophied" is the old Adamist joke). Their numbers are now in decline, as the modified genes which provide resistance to this condition are slowly spread throughout the human gene pool.

Biomechanical systems are used to supplement decaying muscle, bone, and organ tissue. Older cosmoniks (for whom the deteriorating condition is most advanced) have replaced their digestive tract and/or lungs with either artificial tissue or biomechanical organs to replenish the nutrients and oxygen in their blood supply. Skin is usually exchanged for a hard, dark, polymer layer resembling thick leather enabling them to step directly into a vacuum or radiation environment without any other preparation or protection, though hard exoskeleton-type casing can also be used. Many have modified their basic humanoid structure, equipping their feet with gripping claws, giving themselves three forearms each with a specialist tool hand, etc. Most starships carry one or two cosmoniks as crew-members. In extreme cases, a cosmonik will abandon his humanoid form altogether, and transfer his brain into something like a small MSV (multifunction service vehicle). In effect, he then becomes a short-range spacecraft.

Mercenaries

Despite the relatively stable interstellar situation policed by the Confederation, soldiers for hire are still a large business. Although there are no longer any land wars or interstellar invasions, the requirement for limited "special forces" actions is at an all-time high. Asteroid-settlement rebellions against their founding companies are a frequent occurrence, with each side hiring mercenary groups to inflict strategic damage against the other. In the case of the companies, boosted mercenaries are usually employed to temporarily reinforce local police forces, while the rebels use their mercenaries to strike against the company's assets in another star system.

There also occur insurrections on stage-one colony worlds, which fall outside the usual law-enforcement officer remit, allowing the development-company governor to hire professional soldiers to quell the situation. Between such actions, mercenaries are usually employed by the same development companies to act as marshals on stage-one worlds, their specializations making them ideal for the kind of independent tracking necessary at the frontiers of new planets.

Like cosmoniks, this group relies on extensive biomechanical augmentation to achieve their profession's requirements. There is no standardization when it comes to boosting the human form for combat; mercenaries range from fast scouts to what are essentially biological tanks. Most mercenaries start with simple bone strengthening and muscle amplification through either replacement or additional artificial tissue grafts. Sensor enhancement is also a prerequisite, with implants wired directly into neural nanonics. Weapon implants are not so common: boosted mercenaries tend to modify their limbs to accept plug-ins or to improve normal handling characteristics.

Exowombs

Perfected in 2065 so that couples with fertility problems could have children, they were almost immediately adopted by wealthy women to avoid the physical strains of childbirth and the limitations it temporarily placed on their lifestyle. Exowombs played an important role during the divergence of Adamism and Edenism, and still remain important to the expansion of both cultures.

Their first large-scale use was by the Edenists following Eden's declaration of independence in 2090, when they were employed to increase the populations of Eden and Pallas with germ plasma bought from Earth. This breeding program saw the start of comprehensive geneering for Edenists, improving everyone on an equal basis. It was also an opportunity to give every future Edenist an affinity gene.

They are not widely used on Earth in 2600, although

Adamists began utilizing the technology after the onset of interstellar colonization. Exowombs are employed quite extensively by Adamists during the mid-term stage of a planet's colonization. This is when the purely agrarian phase is being left behind and they are moving towards full industrialization, always a time of large expansion and raised horizons. Families of these eras can have typically eight to twelve children without placing repeated childbearing stress on the mother.

Asteroid dwellers and starship crew-members tend to deposit large quantities of germ plasm in storage once they reach adolescence. Radiation exposure during flight is still a problem—certainly accidental exposure—and exowombs give them the opportunity to have "normal" families despite the hazards of their jobs.

Education

On all advanced worlds and asteroid settlements this consists almost entirely of didactic laser memory imprints: subject matter is loaded directly into the brain, the rate being varied according to an individual's ability to absorb it. School for Adamist children consists of a weekly didactic memory-absorption assessment, and then the imprint of a new memory. This leaves children with considerable time on their hands, creating a large industry of day clubs to keep them occupied through organized games and events, and helping to develop their social skills. Basic education is completed at around age sixteen, after which brighter children, nominally 70 percent, have the opportunity to go on to universities, which employ a combination of didactic imprints and traditional tutorial sessions or research projects aimed at developing students' intellects and analytical abilities. For the remainder there are job-related specialization imprint courses, where appropriate, e.g. maintenance and machine operation, which the average citizen will continue to take throughout their working life.

Governments

There are as many variations of government as there are colonies. The Confederation embraces almost every ideology and religious society possible, from interactive democracies to absolute dictatorships, religious ortho-doxies, monarchies, company fiefdoms, anti-tech pas-toral and anarchies, rich and poor. This variety is a source of some perplexity and bemusement to Edenists (and presumably to the Tyrathca and Kiint). However, the vast majority of Adamist governments are demo-cratic republics along the original Western European and North American mold.

Religion

Adamists still follow the major religious beliefs of Christianity, Islam, Hinduism, Buddhism, and Shinto-ism, as well as every minor orthodoxy. On Confedera-tion worlds, types of faith vary in accordance with the ethnic origin of the population. After the unrest experienced on the initial multiethnic colonies, subsequent colonies (post-2130) tended to derive their population from just one ethnic or religious group, thus giving the majority of Confederation planets a single religion, and adherence to it is often an immigration requirement. Sacred cities and shrines such as the Vatican, Mecca, Amaterasu, and Mt. Abu remain the centers of their respective faiths.

Christian evangelical movements and Islamic fundamentalism have declined to negligible proportions; both of these religions have mellowed considerably since the twentieth century, especially among their followers on Earth, and there is even speculation on an eventual total unity, although this must still be several centuries distant.

Of more immediate concern to current religious leaders is the declining numbers of the faithful. The impact of a technological society on the tenets of basic faith has never let up. At the start of the twenty-seventh century, less than 5 percent of the population now attends regular worship. Ironically, on Earth, the most technology-intensive planet in the Confederation, the massive population base supported by the arcologies means that this same 5 percent gives the major religions there a larger following than at any time since the early twentieth century.

The Christian Unification of 2044 means that all Christians now have access to the confessional, priests are both male and female, and celibacy is no longer practiced, while contraception is actually endorsed, especially on Earth.

Cult religions continue to flourish, although these tend to center around their own founder, and diminish after that founder's death unless an even more charismatic successor can be found.

Colonization

Adamists have colonized 861 terracompatible planets, and an average of five new planets are opened up for colonization each year. Settlement rights belong to the discoverer (provided the discovery is filed with the Confederation to establish a legal claim), although most scoutships are owned by either institutions or governments. Establishing a colony is not a cheap proposition, and requires considerable financial backing which few individuals can provide. Thus, independently owned scoutships usually sell on the settlement rights to institutions. The criteria for establishing a settlement are as follows.

Biological clearance

This entails proving that native organisms do not harbor a bacteriological threat. Given the efficiency of today's Adamist immunology systems, it would have to be a highly potent xenoc bacteria or virus which could pose a threat to human life. Only seven newly discovered planets have been disqualified on these grounds in the last hundred years. The existence of native vegetation which has human-compatible protein structure is also a big plus factor in favor of settlement, especially if the species then proves popular, and even more so if the planetary climate is unique (see Norfolk, page 162). Clearance certification is given by the Confederation assessment board, which reviews the results of the ecological analysis team which the owner of the new settlement rights needs to provide. The Confederation does not undertake any analysis work itself.

It is not legally necessary to have Confederation certification before opening a planet to settlement; however, because of the board's impartiality this certificate is a guarantee of safety, and only the most foolhardy of colonists would attempt to settle a planet when certification has not been applied for.

Indigenous sentient species

These are an automatic disqualification for settlement. In the case of a xenoc species which had not yet achieved an industrial-level civilization, further contact is prohibited by the Confederation Assembly in order to prevent cultural contamination. So far only one pre-industrial species has been found: the Jiciro. Confederation Navy monitor satellites have been placed in their star system to monitor compliance with the no-contact law, while universities sponsored by the Assembly maintain a discreet watch on the Jiciro civilization via stealthed low-orbit observation satellites.

Contact with xenocs is automatically permitted when they have a spacefaring technology, although precisely what capability must be demonstrated is subject to debate. A life-support capsule launched into orbit with a chemical rocket is not usually deemed sufficient, whereas regular interplanetary flights are. Discovery of Confederation monitoring systems would also be a valid means of proving technological maturity. The only exception to this rule so far have been the Kiint, who are simply not interested in space travel but whose social and cultural maturity obviously exceeds both Adamist and Edenist levels.

Resources
The mining of planetary mineral resources, with its subsequent environmental contamination, is no longer practiced, thanks to the perfection of cost-effective asteroid mineral-extraction techniques. However, this does mean that a star system must have sufficient asteroids in convenient orbits before the establishment of a technological- and industrial-based colony can be considered. Planets in a star system without an asteroid ring are usually settled by groups searching only for a pastoral existence. There is no legal prohibition against developing planetary surface mining if this pastoral life is rejected at a later date. But disaffected colonists searching for a more technologically advanced culture tend to emigrate to a world with a culture they find more acceptable than farming and base-line manufacturing.

Gas giants
Because of the cost involved in importing He$_3$ to a system which does not have a gas giant, any asteroid settlements in such a system will suffer economic penalties

in comparison to settlements in other systems where He$_3$ is mined, and therefore cheaper (see Edenist Economy, page 39, for the two-tier price system). Therefore a gas giant which can be mined for He$_3$ has become a prerequisite in establishing a (non-pastoral) colony, unless there are exceptional extenuating circumstances. Any institution attempting to set up a system-wide colonization project (apart from the Kulu Kingdom principalities) has to have Edenist cooperation, although this is granted in virtually all cases, provided the founders (normally a development company) can successfully demonstrate the project's viability. Edenists will not help founders who devise a deliberately oppressive constitution.

Constitutions

These are written by the founding group, who may incorporate any doctrine they wish (see Gas giants, above, for Edenist censure). However, as nearly all colonies are now founded by financial concerns, constitutions are designed to encourage industry and commerce in order to pay off the original investment. This tends to negate any restrictive or oppressive charter which would inhibit wealth creation, and of course it has to provide enough incentives—such as free land and low-interest loans—to attract colonists.

Usually the founding institution will form the initial government, which will gradually abrogate its control to the population as the investment is paid off. A timescale for this is often written into the constitution, typically seventy to a hundred years. Even when the institution itself relinquishes political control, it will invariably remain the largest single corporate entity in the star system, and so will continue to generate a return on its investment. It is therefore in the institution's own interest to create a properly working economy.

Asteroid Settlements

Zero-gee industrial stations form an integral part of any star system's technoeconomy. Planets and asteroid settlements need each other in order to trade and enhance their economies, therefore any attempt to colonize a planet with an industrial-based society must also include the establishment of asteroid settlements within the star system.

Asteroid settlements retain a degree of independence from the planetary government, but when full industrialization is achieved a system-wide congress is usually formed to cover defense, criminal extradition, currency regulations, mutual economic policy, transport regulations, etc. (the Edenist habitat will not form part of the congress). It is usually this congress which sends a representative to sit in the Confederation Assembly on Avon, and to speak for the whole star system.

Asteroid settlements use a mix of fusion and solar power, depending on location. They always try to be self-sufficient in food production, using protein vats and hydroponics. The cavern chamber biosphere is usually planted with fruit trees and edible vegetation. Like Edenist habitats, the asteroid settlements provide a healthy market for imported food.

There are two types of—or locations for—asteroid settlements.

High orbit

Typically in orbit 100,000km above the terracompatible planet, these are asteroids with a high metallic content, and have been maneuvered into their orbit by a series of controlled nuclear explosions. They average 30–40km in diameter, and in their first stages provide nothing but raw metal for the planetary industries. The number of asteroids thus captured is in direct proportion to the planet's population, and a newly founded colony will only have one orbiting asteroid for probably the first hundred years. After that, as industrial capacity expands, more asteroids will be captured to feed it. A rough guide to how long a planet has been industrialized is the number of asteroids in its orbit.

Regarding the method of settlement, to begin with a central habitation chamber will be hollowed out of the rock and the whole asteroid given a rotation to provide gravity. Hydrocarbons are then processed to provide a habitable biosphere within the chamber. Because of the cost of shipping in the necessary chemicals, scoutships will always try and locate a metallic asteroid with a smear of hydrocarbons, usually left over from a past collision with a carbonaceous chondritic asteroid.

As the population of an asteroid increases, and the metal ore reserves decline, so the asteroid turns to manufacturing as its principal economic activity. In turn it will start to import raw material, facilitating the capture of new asteroids.

The population of a mature asteroid settlement can reach 100,000, though it rarely exceeds this. Politically, the high-orbit asteroids are nearly always under the control of the planetary government. Certainly this is the case to start with; but as the star system economy develops, companies may well fund their own capture missions and mining settlements.

Free settlements

These can be sited anywhere in the star system, though investors prefer asteroids close enough to the sun to use solar-power arrays, eliminating He_3 costs. Asteroids with large and varied mineral reserves are sought, because of the disparate material requirements of the industrial stations they serve. High-technology zero-gee products are the only exports from these settlements, so they are usually founded several decades after the first batch of colonists arrive on a planet, when a market for their goods is beginning to materialize. Like the mining asteroids in planetary orbit, the habitation chamber is hollowed out of the asteroid itself, providing the inhabitants with several kilometers of rock as protection from cosmic radiation and attacks from mercenary starships. That population is usually around 100,000, although the larger asteroids, containing several habitation chambers, can carry populations as high as 250,000.

In parallel with the institutions that found planetary development, it is companies which finance the construction of asteroid settlements, and their control is never entirely relinquished. All asteroid settlements are essentially company towns. The major (and rare) exception to this is when the star system is being developed by an ideological or religious concern, in which case they will also pay for their own asteroid settlements.

Defense

Attack by mercenary starships is a very real threat for asteroid settlements and planets alike, and all governments fear an assault by a political rival using antimatter. As a consequence, any industrial planet has to devote a healthy percentage of its gross domestic product to building and maintaining a strategic-defense network. Earth's O'Neill Halo defenses are widely regarded as impregnable by any fleet another Confederation world could throw at it.

In combination with the SD network, the major line of defense for any world is its designated emergence zones. As a general rule, starships are not allowed to emerge within 100,000km of an inhabited planet. They are required to jump into the emergence zone, and request flight clearance from the local traffic control authority before approaching their destination, giving naval ships time to perform an inspection when deemed necessary. The SD platforms will shoot at any starship violating this restriction, which is automatically assumed to be on a hostile strike mission.

In wealthy star systems, with a large interplanetary

(non-FTL drive) spaceship fleet shipping products between asteroid settlements and the inhabited planet,
navy ships are on regular patrol to prevent acts of piracy
by starships who can immediately jump out-system as
soon as the looted cargo has been taken on board. It is
this kind of piracy which forms the vast majority of
deep-space crime and, given the lack of supralight communications, is the most successful. With the maneu-
verability of mercenary ships (see Starships, page 57),
even a two-minute response time is often inadequate.
Apart from voidhawks, few navy starships could jump
to the aid of a ship under attack within a quarter of an
hour.

Two

Edenist Culture

The term Edenist derives from the first bitek habitat to be germinated: Eden. It was germinated in Jupiter orbit by the JSKP (Jovian Sky Power Corporation) to provide a dormitory and engineering support facility for its He_3 mining operation within the gas giant's atmosphere. The affinity bond had just been discovered by Wing-Tsit Chong, and all sub-sentient bitek organisms were implanted with a symbiont neuron so that they could receive direct instructions from a human.

Affinity is a silent voice, also capable of carrying a sensorium, similar to classic telepathy. Between individual Edenists it has a range of about 100km. A bitek habitat can receive from and communicate with other habitats, bitek organisms, and Edenists over a 100,000km range. With 4,250 mature habitats orbiting Jupiter, these provide an affinity zone, or relay, across the whole Jovian moon system. The combined Jovian habitats' affinity can communicate with the habitats orbiting Saturn, no matter what their relative orbital positions, and also contact voidhawks within Neptune's orbit (see later for voidhawk affinity ability).

Until 2065 affinity bonds were unique, allowing one person to control just one servitor animal. This was accomplished by using a pair of cloned symbiont neurons, one of which was implanted in a human's brain, the other in the servitor, providing the user with a kind of telepathy.

Such an arrangement was obviously impractical for controlling an entity as vast as a habitat, so Eden itself was given a neural strata which would be sentient, allowing it to regulate and control all its own functions. Wing-Tsit Chong contributed to the project by developing the habitat's thought routines, and by modifying affinity to provide a communal affinity symbiont allowing everyone to converse with both the habitat and each other. He then went on to incorporate the affinity neural architecture into a gene sequence which could be spliced into a fetus, giving a child the same ability from birth. Those children were the first to grow up in this unique environment, sharing their thoughts with each other and with Eden. While not entirely eliminating negative traits such as jealousy, such an atmosphere conducive to honesty and trust greatly reduced them. A hint of what was to come . . .

Without informing the JSKP or the other geneticists involved in the project, Wing-Tsit Chong also designed Eden's neural strata with the capability to receive and run a dying person's thoughts and memories, thus allowing his or her personality to live on after the body's death.

Wing-Tsit Chong was the first person to transfer his memories into the neural strata, when he died in 2090, and in doing so started a rift with the Christian and Muslim faiths which has never been healed.

The affinity gene was declared a violation of divine heritage by Pope Eleanor. Eden then declared independence from the JSKP (see *A Second Chance at Eden*). A similar Islamic proclamation followed swiftly. Pope Eleanor also threatened to excommunicate anyone using symbiont neurons. In the five years following, all the remaining people possessing the affinity gene or symbionts (Christian or otherwise) emigrated to Eden and Pallas. After this, the use of the affinity symbionts and bonded domestic servitor animals died out on Earth. Bitek organisms were also abandoned, leaving bitek as an almost exclusively Edenist technology. By 2110 the dividing line between the two human cultures was fully established.

As well as providing easy communication, affinity is used by children to absorb educational programs from the Eden habitat personality, an equivalent of the Adamist didactic courses. The personality also employs affinity to coordinate the servitor constructs which maintain the central habitat parkland.

Affinity is also used to interface with bitek processor chips, in a similar fashion as does an Adamist neural nanonic datavise to a processor block. Bitek processors are used in all Edenist spaceships and industrial facilities, such as cloudscoops and zero-gee factories. Although all Edenists have the communal affinity trait, private one to one mental conversation is still possible, and cannot be overheard by other Edenists, being called "singular engagement."

Identity Continuity and Habitat Consciousness

When Edenists die, they transfer their memories into the habitat, contributing to the habitat personality. This personality is therefore an assemblage of the habitat's original thought routines and the identities of every Edenist ever to die inside. So, although one entity, the personality is also a multiplicity.

This thought transfer is the principal bone of contention with Adamist religions (particularly Christianity), which consider it an attempt to circumvent divine judgment. This apparent life-continuation, and with it the removal of the human fear of death, is one reason why Edenists are, as a general rule, extremely well-balanced individuals. Also contributing to this enhanced mental health is the communal affinity which allows an Edenist to share and therefore mitigate any personal stress and worry. Cases of insanity or even anxiety attacks are virtually unheard of among Edenists.

Although one distinct entity, the habitat personality is homogenized through the use of thought subroutines running in parallel through the neural strata, allowing it to converse with millions of Edenists all at once as well as running its own nonautonomous functions. Edenists do not necessarily transfer their personalities in the habitat where they were born, only where they die. In the cases of Edenists working outside habitat affinity range, such as diplomats, or passengers in transit, their memories can be stored within a voidhawk's memory cells until they reach a habitat again, when they're transferred into the neural strata.

Transferred personalities remain accessible on an individual level, helping to remove the trauma of parental and grandparental death from children and even from adults. It has been noted that, after a century or so, it becomes difficult to rouse some individual personalities from immersion within the multiplicity. Ultimately the merging becomes irreversible. However, other individuals have been known to retain their complete distinct identity for centuries, most noticeably Wing-Tsit Chong himself.

Genetic Engineering

Edenist life expectancy is currently in excess of 160 years. The Edenists of 2600 are the product of considerable and methodical geneering dating right back to the founding of their culture and, unlike Adamists, their overall modification program is still continuing. Adult Edenists require only four hours of sleep every twenty-four hours, their sensorium clarity is higher, high tolerance to pain is built in, and life expectancy rises a few years with every generation.

One of their major physiological divergences from

the Adamists is the adaptation of Edenist bodies to low- and zero-gee environments because of the large numbers who work outside the habitats in microgee industrial stations. Vertigo and free-fall disorientation have been banished from Edenists; they require no visual horizon reference in zero-gee. Also their bodies are immune to zero-gee atrophy: bones do not waste, blood-cell balance remains unchanged, alterations to veins and capillaries and arteries prevent the pooling of blood in the head, taste and smell are retained at near full sensitivity. This faculty causes them to regard both the boosted and cosmoniks (there are no Edenist cosmoniks) with some pity. The descendants of the hundred families from whom voidhawk crews are traditionally drawn have taken their modification a stage further than the Edenist norm. Their internal membranes are strengthened to hold organs in place during high-gee acceleration, and heart efficiency has been increased to ensure that a regular blood supply is maintained, thus preventing blackouts; they are capable of enduring three gees for days at a time, although this still does not bring them level with the tolerance of boosted blackhawk crews (see Blackhawks, page 63). The largest area of Edenist genetic research is currently concentrated on giving humanity a body immunity to radiation exposure, or at least the ability to recover from it. Although highly resistant to ordinary varieties of cancer, Edenists exposed to high levels of radiation in space remain susceptible to it. Like Adamists, they tend to deposit their germ plasm into storage at the start of their careers.

Atlantian Edenists have received extensive specialist

genetic modification to cope with their unique environment, and are visually easy to identify. Their corium includes extra glands which produce an oil that renders the epidermis water-resistant. The subcutaneous fat layer has been thickened to provide greater thermal insulation. Toe length has been doubled, and they are webbed; fingers are half-webbed. Their blood has a high level of hemoglobin, so they can swim for long periods under water.

Exowombs and Reproduction

Exowombs are used extensively, though not exclusively. Most Edenist women will have one in-body pregnancy, which tends to be when young, aged twenty-one to twenty-five. Further children are gestated inside exowombs. Large families are the norm for Edenist couples. Edenists' children are given considerable physical freedom from an early age. Communal affinity ensures they are never out of contact with their parents, and a habitat interior is an entirely safe environment for a child to roam through, since the habitat personality monitors them (as it does everybody) on a twenty-four-hour basis. Should a child get into difficulty, servitors can be directed to assist immediately.

Edenist sexual mores are a constant source of amusement, speculation, and envy for the Adamists. As they are immune to most diseases, and traits such as (classical) ugliness, obesity, and congenital deformities have been removed from the primary Edenist gene pool, and as communal affinity precludes excessive jealousy or possessiveness, Edenist adolescents lead highly active sex lives. Group sex is common, although this does not replace or prevent normal pairing and love bonding. Most Edenists settle down into a long-term relationship, with compatibility enhanced by affinity. Adamist mythology casts Edenist females in the role of an easy lay, which often leads to considerable friction on a personal level.

Education

Education is received entirely from the habitat via affinity, and is essentially equivalent to the didactic laser imprints of the Adamists, consisting of large chunks of memory/data absorbed by the brain during sleep periods. This procedure is in many ways more advanced than laser didactic imprinting, since the habitat can quiz an individual directly, and very accurately determine which sections of the education memory have been successfully absorbed, then repeat the missing sections until full understanding of a subject is reached. In this fashion, talent and aptitude can be developed to maximum potential, be it in arts or science.

Morals or behavioral traits are also included in this education process. That's an aspect which Adamists object to strongly, claiming it is little more than ideological conditioning. It does mean that crime in Edenist habitats is almost unheard of. Edenists do not take drugs (including tobacco), although they will drink alcohol (their liver and kidneys eradicate the worst aspects of a hangover), but rarely to excess once they reach maturity, nor do they use sensevise stims. Sexual activity is the Edenists' preferred method of obtaining a high.

Culture

Despite their indoctrination, education, and apparent conformity (to outside eyes) to their own culture, Edenists are highly individualistic. They can, and frequently do, disagree with each other, though this takes the form of "agree to disagree" rather than any kind of hateful confrontation or political wrangling. Normal (sic) human traits remain present, giving their society the usual artistic-practical divisions. Edenists are by no means equal, though they claim to have no social strata. The habitats' ubiquitous bitek servitors contribute greatly to this situation, by eliminating mundane physical labor. There is no working class in an Edenist habitat, or poverty either.

Religion

None, since all Edenists are atheists.

Serpents

When an Edenist goes bad, they go all the way, so the saying goes. There are a very few Edenists who will reject their culture after all the educational techniques and therapeutic counseling available to them. Those that do are referred to, with some irony, as "Serpents." Statistically this occurs to approximately just one in 15m, and is a considerable source of embarrassment to the rest of the Edenist population. Although affinity can open their minds to one another, the sharing of thoughts cannot be forced. Serpents shut themselves off from communal affinity, and invariably leave the habitat of their birth. They nearly always drift into quasi-legal—or actively illegal—activities, presumably in reaction to the very moralistic culture in which they have been raised.

To add to the embarrassment of Edenists, the Serpents, with their high intelligence and relish for challenge, tend to be highly successful in these nefarious fields. The independent bitek habitat Valisk was germinated by Rubra, and remains the Confederation's premier example of Serpent achievement, though Rubra was something of an exception. Serpents in general bend towards infamy, and in more extreme cases to outright evil.

Converts

A slow but steady stream of about 1,000,000 Adamist converts join the Edenist culture each year, though notably not from the ranks of the religiously devout. They are given neuron symbionts so they can take part in communal affinity, and specialist tutors help them make the mental adjustments necessary. One of their major reasons for joining is the life-continuity granted by transferring memories into the habitat at death. Nobody is ever refused Edenist status, and a surprising 91 percent of converts make a successful adaptation. Genetically their absorption poses no problem, as 85 percent of Adamists already have geneering in their heritage, and the all-important affinity gene becomes dominant, so that the offspring of any Edenist Adamist pairing is always a true Edenist.

Converts tend to be young, under thirty, since older people have trouble adapting. Over a third of converts join because of romantic attachments they have developed with individual Edenists. Sixty percent of these cases involve voidhawk crew-members, leading to the Edenist claim that the hundred families have "wild blood." As yet there have been no xenoc converts to Edenism, though should any ever apply they would not be refused.

Government

Edenism can be regarded as a super-consensus democracy, in which every single individual not only votes but takes part in forming policy. The Consensus is the collective consciousness of all Edenists living within a habitat, joined through affinity and acting in concert. It is normally called into session once every year, to review policy and mandate new laws. In practice there have been few new laws introduced to Edenism in the last two centuries.

Consensus exists at many levels. All the habitats in orbit around one of the gas giants will normally join together to form a total Consensus. Sub-Consensus also exists within a habitat personality to monitor various situations or activities, such as security and defense, which might require urgent and immediate decisions. Sub-Consensus members are drawn from the multiplicity of living Edenists who have the relevant experience in these fields. Though they can act with considerable autonomy, they are ultimately responsible to the Consensus itself.

Each habitat has an elected administrator, and elections are held every five years. No individual may serve more than three terms, and anyone may put his or her name forward. The position of habitat administrator is largely ceremonial, dating back to the founding, as the habitat personality itself performs every administrative detail, eradicating the need for a civil-service bureaucracy. He or she is also the representative to whom Adamist ambassadors are appointed, and is responsible for diplomatic relations with the Adamists and Confederation in general. In effect, these administrators form Edenism's diplomatic corps. The administrator also has some legal power, including the authority to repeal habitat personality judgments (see Law, below).

Law

Because every Edenist is committed to a common ideal of civil behavior, there is very little illegal activity. Indeed there is little point in anyone trying to commit a crime, since the habitat consciousness becomes instantly aware of every activity within its interior. Cutting corners when under pressure and heat-of-the-moment rashness are the most common offenses. And it is interesting to note that most of these occur *outside* the habitat. The habitat personality serves the role of judge and jury. Informal warnings are the norm, and a formal public rebuke from the habitat personality is normally punishment enough to prevent any repetition. However, for persistent offenders an ever increasing scale of fines, as well as leisure-time restrictions, is available.

For extremely serious crimes (there have only been five murders in 500 years of Edenist history within Edenist domains), a habitat personality will prevent a convict from any external travel, in effect imprisoning them inside the habitat, and the ultimate sanction is to refuse to accept that individual's memories at death. An Edenist has the right of appeal to the habitat administrator against any such judgment.

Only a direct order from the administrator can reverse or reduce these sentences, and a habitat personality must accept the administrator's decision. This man-in-the-loop failsafe was included right at the start of Edenism, when the nature of a habitat personality was not fully understood, and Eden's multiplicity had not properly developed. It has never been removed, since Edenists and habitat personalities alike acknowledge that humans must have such a psychological safety valve. An administrator will typically use this power of revocation twice every ten years, though it has never been used to pardon a really serious crime.

Currency

The Edenist unit of currency is officially the dollar, though it is now referred to entirely as the fuseodollar. It is the strongest, most prevalent currency in the Confederation, remaining stable since 2135, and as such has become the standard against which every other currency is measured. With one or more habitats in most of the Confederation's 862 inhabited systems (the principal exception being the Kulu Kingdom), and the infallibility and incorruptibility of the habitat consciousness which handles all fuseodollar transactions, Edenism has become through the Jovian Bank the premier interstellar banking institution.

The Jovian Bank has branches on a large proportion of planets and asteroid settlements throughout the Confederation (including the Kulu Kingdom), and all major multi-stellar organizations (such as the Confederation civil service) use the Edenist dollar as their currency.

Economy

The foundation of Edenist wealth comes from mining He_3, the fuel used in fusion reactors throughout the Confederation primarily because of its clean burning qualities (low neutron emission) when combined with deuterium. Not only is it used for commercial power generation on- and off-planet, it is the principal drive system of all Adamist starships, both interstellar and interplanetary. The cloudscoop mining operation of gas giants, around which the habitats orbit, is considered to be owned by all Edenists equally, and its finance is administered by the habitat personality (see Finance, below).

The price of He_3 remains the same throughout the Confederation, even in systems where there is no cloudscoop operation, and that price has remained stable for 500 years. Although not a pure monopoly, the Edenist operation is so large that anyone else running a cloudscoop operation is forced to supply He_3 at the same rate.

When Eden and Pallas declared independence from the UN in 2090, they also initiated a (hostile) buy-out of the JSKP multinational consortium which had originally funded Jupiter's atmospheric mining. Because of the enormous cost involved in starting up the operation, the debt was not paid off until 2135. After this the Edenists were truly independent. Fusion remains the major power source throughout the Confederation and, given the gas giant reserves of He_3, is likely to remain so. Research continues into direct mass-to-energy conversion and other systems, but as yet none has demonstrated any practical application. Following the one serious attempt to break the Edenist energy monopoly, when Earth built antimatter stations, Confederation politicians have retained a policy of quiet moderation in this field.

The continuing demand for He_3, and their use of self-sufficient bitek habitats, means that as a group Edenists have the highest socioeconomic index in the Confederation. It is worth noting that even if He_3 fusion were completely abandoned by the Confederation, their bitek habitats, financial services, and industrial strength would mean that Edenists could retain their standard of living with little disturbance. Although Adamists complain bitterly among themselves about the He_3 monopoly (excepting the Kulu Kingdom and Tranquillity) they also acknowledge that the Edenists, with their high ethical standards, are an ideal group to supply the Confederation with this fuel. Political blackmail is not an option ever considered by Edenists, even as regards the most oppressive Adamist dictatorships. Edenists regard the Confederation Assembly and its Navy as the only legitimate method of censure.

Finance

The habitat personality acts as bank and accountant for all financial transactions, corporate or personal. There is no physical cash in the form of notes and coins, and the fuseodollar is an entirely electronic currency, distributed through Jovian Bank credit disks.

Although Edenism is certainly not a Communist ideology, revenue raised from He$_3$ mining is administered by the habitat personality, and made available on a communal basis; a research project or an artistic endeavor considered worthwhile, for example, will be funded from this central source. Capital for commercial enterprises is also advanced by the Jovian Bank. Edenists do not seek funding from Adamist banks, which is another source of contention, as Adamists frequently apply for loans from the Jovian Bank. Because of affinity, the habitat personality (through its financial sub-Consensus) is actively involved in the planning of commercial ventures from conception through to researching marketability, etc., so that when a project reaches the stage where finance is necessary to fund start-up manufacturing, it will always be granted.

Industry

Edenism is technologically and industrially self-sufficient, and the habitat-based companies export a great quantity of manufactured products across the Confederation. Problems with radiation shielding aside, gas-giant orbits are an ideal place to site zero-gee industrial stations, providing proximity to supplies of raw material, energy, and habitat populations. Jupiter is the greatest concentration of manufacturing capacity in the Confederation, even managing to out-produce Earth's O'Neill Halo. Edenist companies tend to be run on a family level (extended family), with executive ownership spread among participating members; primary funding always comes from the Jovian Bank. Children of participants are eligible to work their way in after they reach legal maturity (at age nineteen).

Trade

The relative wealth of the citizenship, plus a prodigious appetite for luxury goods and exotic food make Edenist habitats an extremely valuable market for the Confederation, and commerce is correspondingly brisk. Adamist starship companies rarely have any complaints about Edenists in public or private, as their habitats, right across the Confederation, provide a huge market. Although He_3 is Edenism's main export, their high-technology astroengineering industries are also extremely competitive, and sell throughout the Confederation. Even though He_3 is carried almost exclusively by voidhawks and Edenist-owned tankers, the shipment of manufactured goods is put out to free tender, and Adamist starships obtain a high percentage of the contracts. There are over 20,000 starship movements daily in the Jovian system, making it the busiest sector in the Confederation.

Habitats

These are bitek cylinders of living, highly modified coral (polyp), always found in orbit around gas giants. All Edenists live in these enclaves, with the exception of Atlantis (see page 53). In the Jovian system they orbit

550,000km above the planet, which puts them above the orbit of Io and its lethal flux tube and hazardous ion torus, but they keep well within the planetary magnetosphere, thus giving them a sidereal period of about two days.

They are grown from seeds (teardrop shaped, approximately 150m long and 50m wide), which are manufactured in specialist bitek stations, and are the largest artificial creatures ever designed (voidhawks and blackhawks claim to be more sophisticated). A new seed will be removed from its manufacturing station and germinated before being attached to a small asteroid (1km diameter) which contains appropriate trace minerals to support its initial growth phase. The first stage of germination produces a membrane which envelopes the entire asteroid, and then digestion begins inside. The membrane is flooded with enzyme fluid to break up the minerals, and these are reabsorbed by a root network. Minerals and organic compounds are processed inside the seed by rudimentary organs, and so polyp growth begins.

Once the basic cylinder shape is achieved, after four to six years, the seed and membrane sac digestive mechanism withers away and disengages. The cylinder at this point is 2km long, and is little more than an empty shell with a more sophisticated digestive system at one end. A new asteroid is maneuvered into its maw (a hemispherical indentation at one end, covered with spine-like cilia), and the primary digestion process begins. Growth to full size takes up to thirty years, and several asteroids are ingested during this time.

Layout and Composition

The first habitat to be germinated, Eden itself, is 10km long and 3km wide; the second, Pallas, is 15km long and 5km wide. Both are still alive, as cellular regeneration is constant provided the maw is fed with raw material. More modern habitats are up to 45km long and 10km wide, with hemispherical endcaps, and an external ring of starscrapers around the center. They rotate along their long axis to provide a 0.9 gravity field in the park, and a standard Earth gravity at the base of the starscrapers. Each habitat will typically house up to 2,000,000 people. The shell is 500m thick in total, which is more than sufficient to protect the inhabitants from Jupiter's (and all other gas giants') hostile radiation environment.

The external layer is made up from a crust of dead polyp 20m thick, which is gradually abraded away by particle impacts and vacuum ablation, though there are several surface sections of living sensitive cells which allow the habitat to "see" its surroundings. These cells receive and interpret a wide section of both the electromagnetic and magnetic spectrum, as well as being sensitive to elementary particles. The outer layer is constantly replenished from the first living polyp layer, which is nothing more than a sheath of living rock.

Above this is the extremely complex mitosis layer where the polyp is produced for the habitat's interior and exterior. The mitosis layer is webbed with nutrient ducts fed from the maw digestive mechanism and organs; there are several distinct duct networks, each supplying a specialist fluid. Inward from the mitosis layer is the equally elaborate environment-support layer, which maintains the internal atmosphere, distributing oxygen, nitrogen, and water, which come from dedicated organs in the endcap. There are several reservoirs of each element, spaced at regular intervals throughout the shell. This layer also contains carbon dioxide filters to back up the vegetation in the cavern, while subsidiary filters eliminate any build-up of poisonous or toxic gas, and help purify the water.

Above the environmental layer is a tough sandwich layer where polyp encases the neural strata. The millions of homogenized thought routines which make up the habitat consciousness reside in the neural strata, which is affinity-capable. All biological aspects of the habitat are regulated from here, including autonomic functions; it also acts as an overall controller for the servitors.

Above the neural strata, a thick inner layer of polyp is contoured to produce a landscape for the central chamber. In the sections which break through the soil, providing imitation rock, paths, parkland structures, etc., the polyp is overlaid with sensitive cells giving the personality a comprehensive view of the interior. The polyp surfaces of the starscrapers are also suffused with sensitive cells.

Soil is spread over the internal layer, to a depth of several meters, supporting standard plant growth. There is a gentle gradient of 50m between the two ends of the chamber, with the lower finishing in a large circumfluous lake. Water is taken from the lake and pumped back to the higher end via channels lined with peristaltic muscles; it is released into the head of all the streams as well as being injected directly into the deep soil layers, allowing a constant circulation and irrigation across the chamber.

Starscrapers

Starscrapers are tower-like accommodation sections, up to 500m long, which protrude from the central section of the habitat, forming an equatorial band. There are windows on every level, giving spectacular views over the gas giants and their moon systems, and these are all fitted with irises which close during radiation storms. Essentially they are vertical towns, containing every civic amenity from individual apartments to theaters, with shops, bars, and offices included. Most Edenists live inside a habitat's starscraper, given that there are few other internal structures; Edenists like to keep the chamber parkland unspoiled. The main exceptions to this rule are the habitats in orbit around Saturn, which have no starscrapers because of the higher particle density that makes them susceptible to damage (Saturn habitats have much thicker external shell layers).

All starscraper apartments are provided with food-synthesis organs, providing a steady if monotonous diet of fruit juice and paste-like protein-rich hydrocarbons of various flavors. Secretion teats are provided in every apartment wall. Human excrement is carried away through a digestive tract, and reprocessed in organ clusters at the base of the tower, while harmful toxins are vented through porous sections of the shell. The food organs are not widely used, since Edenists favor cooking food (there is no butchery—meat is grown in clone vats), and import a great many delicacies from across the Confederation. This waste matter finds its way directly into the ecosystem via the digestive tracts.

Power

Most of the biological processes within the habitat's major organs utilize variants of electrolysis and ion-exchange mechanisms, rather than straightforward biochemical reactions. This reduces the dependence on fresh chemicals to a considerable degree, cutting down on the amount of minerals which have to be ingested. Though its chemical consumption is still prodigious, a habitat's main power source is electricity. This energy is generated by simple induction from Jupiter's (and other gas giants') colossal magnetosphere.

Hundreds of specialist extrusion glands are situated around the rim at each end of the cylinder, producing 50m, lengths of organic conductor cabling. Because of the habitat's rotation the cables extend straight outward and slice through the magnetosphere's flux lines. (This means that spacecraft have to approach every habitat along the rotation axis.) Cables are grown on a more or less constant basis, as dust impacts continually weaken them and breakage is frequent. As well as indigenous organ functions and maintaining the environment temperature, the cables provide electricity for domestic use and the light-industry plants situated in the endcaps.

Habitats have a large reserve of electricity stored in electroplaque cells to cope with the fluctuations caused by cable breaks, and in emergencies fusion generators can be plugged directly into the power circuits. Without this pick-up system it is difficult to see how an organism like a habitat could survive, given the amount of energy it requires to heat, light and feed its inhabitants. Photosynthetic membranes, as well as being extremely inefficient, would be impossibly cumbersome on the scale required to provide an equivalent amount of energy.

Light

Electrophorescent cell clusters are used throughout the skyscrapers, although inhabitants are free to redecorate by using electric lighting (chandeliers and lasersolids are popular). The central cavern is illuminated by a column of fluorescent gas contained inside a webbed tube of organic conductors extending down the length of the axis. The web's magnetic field confines the ionized gas, which is constantly fluoresced by a high-voltage discharge. During the night-time period, the luminosity is reduced to the light level of a full (Earth) moon. Repairs to the web are conducted during this period by bitek servitors specially designed to be resistant to the high magnetic flux level and energized gas; these creatures resemble giant spiders with a hard dermal layer.

Climates

Most types of climate exist in the habitats orbiting Jupiter, although Alaskan or Siberian winters are not easily simulated because of the thermal-flow problems this would create inside the shell. A Mediterranean-style climate is the most popular, followed by temperate or tropical. Several temperature habitats grown in the last 150 years have included an atmospheric vapor dispersion system supposed to create occasional snowfalls, though this has met with only moderate success. Eight Jupiter-orbiting habitats are dedicated nature reserves for rare original-genotype Earth animals, plants, and insects (for whales see Atlantis, page 53), with many species reconstructed from stored genetic samples taken in the late twentieth and early twenty-first centuries. One of the most successful reconstructions has been the mammoth cloned from frozen samples found in Siberia.

Mechanical Systems

Bitek is unable to accommodate every requirement, especially moving systems which are subject to constant abrasive use, and in particular transport mechanisms. Lifts are installed in all the starscrapers after they have been grown, and large tunnels are included in the internal polyp land-contour layer for the maglev trains. Cars and powered bikes are also used in the cavern, but only by service crews and medical emergency personnel. Cycling is popular, as is microlight flying and horse riding.

Spaceport

As one end of the habitat is devoted to the maw, space-ship activity is concentrated entirely around the other end. On all post-2220 habitats, the endcap has a series of broad projecting ledges for voidhawks to land on. These rings are studded with pedestals which contain nutrient-fluid transfer mechanisms for the bitek star-ships; fluid-production organs are found in the endcap walls.

All Adamist starships and reaction-drive craft use a counter-rotating spaceport (none of them can perform the kind of swoop maneuver necessary to use a ledge), which extends out from the habitat axis on a long spin-dle. These are the same as spaceports on settled aster-oids, though larger in scale, and can be any shape, from simple extensions of the spindle to discs, globes, and starfish grids. The only thing they have in common is that they are joined to the habitat by a rotating seal at the axis.

Defense

As with Confederation planets and asteroid settlements, starships are not allowed to emerge within 100,000km of a habitat, and they have designated emergence zones. In Jupiter's case, starships are effectively banished from emerging inside Europa's orbit. After emergence, dock-ing authorization and flight-vector management is han-dled by the habitat personality, which is linked into strategic-defense platforms via bitek processor chips.

All industrial stations are maintained within the same orbit as the habitats, which simplifies the job of the strategic-defense platforms. Because Jupiter's gravity field makes emergence impossible closer than 100,000km, the He_3 cloudscoops are relatively safe from direct attack by emerging starships; nevertheless, they are protected by beam weapons mounted on the anchor asteroid. In addition to strategic-defense platforms, there are fifty armed voidhawks on permanent patrol above Jupiter. This situation is repeated, though on a much smaller scale, around every Edenist habitat throughout the Confederation.

Voidhawk Base Habitats

A slight misnomer, as voidhawks are rarely based at Saturn. The 268 habitats in orbit around Saturn serve as an industrial center, nursery, crew-training academy and retirement home for the hundred families. They orbit 300,000km above Saturn, just outside the rings, and deploy the same kind of magnetosphere pick-up cables used by Jupiter-orbiting habitats. The most visible external difference is the lack of starscrapers; instead people live in polyp residences inside the cavern. As a consequence, their population is lower than inside their habitats, with 500,000 residents maximum.

The industrial stations based at Saturn are primarily involved in astroengineering; in constructing and maintaining the voidhawk life-support quarters and cargo bay, as well as building ancillary craft such as ground-to-orbit flyers. There is also a considerable armaments division, providing combat wasps for voidhawks on duty with the Confederation Navy and for habitat defense duties.

Saturn is not the only gas giant whose rings provide suitable nesting grounds for voidhawks. Both Corellstal and Bagarasnin have ring systems which are used by Edenists to propagate voidhawks, though Saturn still produces the majority of these ships.

The Hundred Families

Thus are named the original commercial enterprises involved with developing voidhawks, and the term now refers to both the voidhawk and human branches of the endeavor. On its human side each family is basically a loosely tied merchant house trading as it pleases, with He_3 contracts distributed on an equal basis. Their combined fleet strength is currently in excess of 400,000 voidhawks.

Originally there were only a hundred different types of voidhawk—one each per family. But genetic refinement by Saturn's bitek laboratories as well as crossbreeding has improved the species considerably. New improvements are still being made, with most of the research focusing on how to extend the life of the patterning cells and therefore the overall lifespan.

The humans of the hundred families have undergone extensive geneering to adapt their bodies for prolonged periods of spaceflight. Although they don't have to endure the kind of free-fall exposure experienced by

Adamist starship crews, they have nonetheless followed similar lines of physiological development, and given themselves physiques resistant to atrophy and organ decay, capable of withstanding high-gee acceleration, and immunity to zero-gee sickness. They do not suffer from spatial disorientation, although like all humans they prefer a visual horizon; and they have a high level of radiation cancer immunity.

After a voidhawk matures, the family will fund construction of its mechanical systems, which the captain will pay off, typically, in ten to fifteen years. There is no formal requirement to serve in the Confederation Navy, though most captains chose to serve at least one tour of duty, lasting seven years.

Voidhawk crews are traditionally chosen from Saturn's indigenous population, though not exclusively.

The Atlantis Islands

The only actual planet colonized by Edenists is Atlantis, which is completely oceanic, there being no land mass at all. The inhabitants live on floating bitek islands of polyp, 2km in diameter, typically supporting three major accommodation towers, various civic buildings, and a central park. Six hundred and fifty such islands have been grown so far, each capable of supporting a population of 6,000, and they are a derivative of the original orbital habitat technology. They do not have food-synthesis glands other than for purifying water, but given the abundance of food in the surrounding ocean such a system would be completely irrelevant. They are not equipped with any form of propulsion, and simply drift where the current takes them. However, if one island were to be caught in the polar region for too long, the inhabitants would use tugs to tow it out into a current which would take it back into a warmer climate.

Energy is provided from a combination of systems. One is photosynthesis, where every external surface is covered in a layer of photosynthetic cells, helping to supply the essential organs with nutrients, although this is very much a secondary system. Another is organic thermal-exchange cables, which dangle below the island as it drifts along, exploiting the temperature difference between the surface and bottom of the ocean to generate an electric current; this energy is mainly used by the mechanical and electronic systems in the accommodation towers. The main supply of chemicals for the organs to synthesize comes via large external gills that ingest plankton. These provide enough raw material to sustain the island's polyp structure, and maintain its growth.

Economy

The small amount of industry on these islands is almost solely concerned with shipbuilding. There is a respectable tourist trade, split fifty-fifty between Adamists and Edenists, both of whom seem to find the prospect of a planetary ocean exceptionally challenging. Many come to view the whales, which were introduced into the ocean in 2420. Several luxury cruise ships sail a random course between the floating islands, and many keen sailors hire yachts to circumnavigate the globe.

However, the original reason for establishing the islands is the fishing industry; Atlantis fish and seaweed are delicacies recognized throughout the Confederation, and the planet has eight orbiting stations to cope with visiting trader starships. Each island has several family fishing fleets, and runs surface-to-orbit cargo flyers. After 250 years, it is estimated that only 25 percent of the indigenous aquatic species has been categorized.

Three

Starships and Weapons

The starships fall into three distinct categories: voidhawks, blackhawks and Adamist starships.

Voidhawks

Used exclusively by Edenists, voidhawks are living bitek starships grown around a vast array of energy-patterning cells that can focus energy density until it approaches infinity, distorting local space to such a degree that a wormhole will open through which it can transit. Because the wormhole opens ahead of the voidhawk's track (rather than around it, as with Adamist starships) this maneuver is called the swallow. Transit down a wormhole takes several seconds, and the maximum external range is fifteen light-years. A voidhawk is instinctively aware of its spatial location in relation to star positions, and knows how to "angle" the distortion in order to direct the wormhole's vector and thus produce a terminus at the required point in space.

Propulsion

Acceleration through normal space is achieved by generating a distortion zone below the threshold necessary to open a wormhole, so allowing the ship to ride a distortion wave. Gravity in the crew quarters is generated by a secondary manipulation of this distortion, and it can be produced even when the ship is not under acceleration. There is no theoretical limit to the acceleration a voidhawk can achieve in normal space. But, in practical terms, generating a simultaneous counter-acceleration force for the crew is extremely difficult above 3 gees. As voidhawk crew have been geneered to withstand high-gee acceleration for a considerable time, 6 gees is the standard acceleration for emergency or combat flying, although brief periods of very high gees (10–15) are endurable.

Operating Parameters

No voidhawk can operate from a planetary surface; gravitational force exerts too strong an influence on space for the distortion field to retain its integrity. Although able to orbit planets, a voidhawk's ability to generate a distortion field is severely limited in proportion to altitude, with a typical *lower* limit of 100km above a terracompatible planet; nor can it create a wormhole within 2,000km of a standard-sized terracompatible planet (Adamist starships cannot translate within 5,000km), or 100,000km of a Jovian-size gas giant (Adamist starships 175,000km).

The distortion effect can be used to prevent an Adamist starship from translating, by setting up interference patterns in the distortion field which the Adamist starship's jump nodes generate. A voidhawk can project a distortion zone powerful enough to prevent an Adamist starship's translation, from a distance of 100,000km in clear space. The jump distortion signature of any Adamist ship within a voidhawk's detection range can be read, allowing the voidhawk to follow and intercept. It is these two functions which make voidhawks an essential component of the Confederation Navy.

Structure

Voidhawks are typically lenticular in shape, 120m in diameter and 30m wide at the center. Upper and lower surfaces have an indented groove 10m wide, 5m deep, with a circumference of 60m in diameter, into which its mechanical systems are fitted. The crew quarters form a toroid equipped with cabins, lounges, a gym, a medical center, and the hangar deck for an atmospheric flyer and small atmospheric craft and an MSV; it has its own fusion power supply (triplicated) with fuel-storage tanks, and reserves of oxygen, nitrogen, and water; the life-support systems are bitek organs. The under groove is fitted with cargo-pod and/or combat-wasp cradles.

Internally a voidhawk is a solid mass of cells; by volume 20 percent of these cells is given over to digestive functions (voidhawks consume a hydrocrabon nutrient fluid available from all habitats and most asteroids), neural activity, sensors, nutrient circulation, and reproduction. The remaining 80 percent is energy-patterning cells, which generate the spatial distortion field. Once a voidhawk reaches maturity these energy-patterning cells decay at a rate which cannot be matched by regeneration, and it is this decay which dictates the lifetime of a voidhawk.

Power

Power generation is yet another function of the distortion field, which acts as a lens for cosmic radiation. The patterning cells store their own energy, and can absorb the electromagnetic waves directly. A voidhawk is constantly absorbing energy, and can sustain acceleration through normal space indefinitely, as it expends less energy to generate the distortion than it absorbs from the distortion. However, generating a wormhole requires a large quantity of energy. It takes five hours to accumulate enough energy for one swallow, and the cells can only store enough for at most twelve consecutive swallows, depending on the length of the wormholes generated.

Voidhawks used in Confederation Navy service courier duty have additional fusion generators fitted in their cargo bays to supplement their range, charging the patterning cells directly, although power from this source still requires time to be distributed correctly throughout the patterning cells—twenty minutes per swallow. With or without additional power sources, voidhawks can easily out-perform Adamist starships in most combat situations. Their only real challenge comes from blackhawks.

Reproduction

Artificial production of voidhawk eggs is now very rare, as very few refinements are being incorporated. The Saturn habitat geneticists are working primarily on methods to increase the gravitational counter-acceleration force which voidhawks generate around the crew quarters in order to give them a higher acceleration in normal space, and on extending their life expectancy. If successful, batches of eggs incorporating these improvements will be developed, and these new traits will gradually feed into the main flock. Otherwise, reproduction now follows the cycle originally designed into the species.

Voidhawks only reproduce once. Each craft has eight to twelve eggs stored in its central section, which are hatched in the hours preceding its death. All voidhawks know when their patterning cells are faltering, and they return to Saturn to die. The first act of germination is to load a human zygote into the egg, which includes a womb analogue and hematopoiesis organs. This zygote is always the offspring of the captain and his or her mate(s); the twelve zygotes can be produced at any time, and are stored in zero-tau, waiting for egg germination. After this act the voidhawk is abandoned by its crew, and it flies down towards Saturn. It then absorbs a large quantity of energy from the planet's radiation field, which is used to energize the eggs inside.

The mating flight through the innermost rings which follows involves other voidhawks—as many as are available at Saturn—following the dying craft, and downloading their compositional paradigms (the software equivalents of DNA) via affinity. The paradigms are incorporated into the eggs, and used to format the cellular structure of the new voidhawks. As only the most agile voidhawks can catch up with a craft on its mating flight, this ensures that the breed is strengthened each time. Once every egg has been energized and loaded with a paradigm, they are ejected into orbit, and the parent voidhawk falls into the planet's atmosphere to burn up.

The egg which is left behind begins life as a two-section unit: the infant voidhawk and a nutrient-production segment. This segment is what supports the voidhawk during the eighteen years required for it to reach maturity. It has organic conductor cables similar to those of a habitat to generate energy, and the weak magnetic field it produces gathers in the planet's ring particles for digestion. Its organs convert this ice and carbon dust into usable proteins that then feed the growing voidhawk. They also support the infant captain for the first twelve months of gestation, allowing an exceptionally strong love bond to be established between the two. After this first year, the infant is removed and taken back to the habitat.

A voidhawk lives for its captain, and although it will

accept flight instructions from other Edenists it will only do so if it perceives these instructions to be in the captain's interest. Voidhawk maturity is achieved at eighteen years, at which time its mechanical systems are fitted, and it begins service. Voidhawk affinity range is the greatest in the Edenist genealogy, typically reaching 30AU. Life expectancy is 110 years.

Blackhawks

Bitek starships were initially derived from voidhawks by Rubra, the owner of Valisk, to be used by his company Magellanic Itg as its transport fleet. Several were sold to Adamists outside Rubra's family line, and some were allegedly constructed by quasi-legal biotechnology companies across the Confederation. Origins are notoriously hard to pin down, though Tropicana's involvement in their development is widely acknowledged. Although undoubtedly originating from voidhawk stock (see Valisk, page 208), blackhawks come in a variety of shapes, though there is unlikely to be any truth in the rumor that xenoc games have been spliced into the eggs at some time.

The commonest blackhawk profile is an onion shape, although lozenges, spheres, tapering cylinders and even rings have been seen. One of the reasons for this divergence (or evolution) from the voidhawk norm is alterations spliced in to give the blackhawks an improved combat performance. Although nominally listed as independent traders, blackhawk captains pick up their major income by hiring themselves out as mercenaries, certainly in their early flight years.

Blackhawks have a much larger swallow range than their cousins, typically twenty light-years, allowing them to jump easily out of navy voidhawk interception range—although they can only store enough energy to perform six to eight of these jumps sequentially. They can also maneuver with high agility, but like voidhawks they are not able to protect their crew from continuous acceleration above 3–4 gees. However, most blackhawk crewmembers have nanonic-boosted bodies specifically designed for high-gee resistance, allowing typical combat speeds of 10–15 gees to be sustained over long periods.

Blackhawks use the five independent habitats as bases for their mating flights, and the eggs are sold to the highest bidder. The blackhawk captains do not have the affinity gene, and instead use neuron symbionts to bond with the ships—essentially duplicating the strong bond that exists between voidhawks and their captains; although, given that blackhawk captains will be much older when the process starts, this puts a somewhat different slant on the relationship in that the blackhawk is heavily influenced by its captain's personality. Blackhawk captains tend to stay in the base habitat while the blackhawk matures.

Blackhawk life expectancy is around seventy-five years. The exact numbers of blackhawks in the Confederation is unknown, but there are probably around 10,000 currently operating; the exact figure is difficult to determine because their registration is frequently changed, and some fly with false CAB certificates.

Adamist Starships

Over 1,000,000 ZTT (zero temporal transit) starships are currently in service. They use solid-state jump nodes to generate a wormhole by distorting space directly around the ship. Nodes are energized from onboard fusion generators and then discharged into the patterning circuitry, which creates the distortion by focusing energy density until it becomes infinite. The nodes are arranged in a spherical lattice around the hull, a geometry which creates the wormhole interstice around the ship. In order to function correctly, the distortion must be perfectly symmetrical, so that the force it exerts on the starship is completely balanced. If the nodes are not positioned equidistantly, or the discharge is not simultaneous, then the resulting asymmetrical distortion will rip the ship apart in a spectacularly violent fashion.

The compression effect of imploding infinite-density loci is often powerful enough to initiate fusion within the ship's atoms. This is also the reason why starships cannot jump when they are inside a planet's (or star's) gravity field; a strong gravitational gradient will warp the distortion field into instability. The nodes always have a small error-compensation ability built in so that the inevitable minute discrepancies in geometry and discharge timing do not pose any danger, and ensure that a node failure in deep space is survivable, by al-

lowing a starship to complete its voyage with one or two
defunct units.

FTL Drive Operation

When the node energy discharge is triggered, an event
horizon envelops the starship and it translates virtually
instantaneously, the wormhole terminus expanding at
the same rate as the initiation end collapses, typically
.005 seconds. Orbital trajectory is maintained along the
transit, i.e. the starship jumps along its course vector.
Attempts to equip Adamist starships with nodes that can
duplicate the tailored wormhole vector which voidhawks generate have so far been unsuccessful, since
solid-state systems simply cannot match bitek for complexity; and by volume the voidhawks are 80 percent
energy-patterning cells, while the node mass of an
Adamist starship is typically 7 percent. However, research programs continue, most notably in the Kulu
Kingdom.

Astrogation

Starships will nearly always use a planet to align themselves in preparation for an interstellar jump, this
method allowing considerable time and fuel to be saved.
This maneuver is particularly beneficial when departing
an asteroid settlement.

The measure of a ship's performance is termed its
delta-V, which equates to the total velocity change
which it is capable of making. However efficient a star-

ship's fusion drive, it would have to expend a considerable amount of its delta-V reserve in order to insert itself into an orbit which will intersect its target star, especially if that star is not in the section of space directly ahead of the asteroid. To get around this the starship will perform a small interplanetary jump to the nearest planet. Once in orbit, and when the appropriate inclination has been achieved, the starship's vector will be aligned on the target star once during every revolution. Considerable precision is required to initiate the jump at precisely the correct moment, as even a half-second error will result in a large wormhole terminus location discrepancy, which will have to be countered before the second jump is initiated.

With typical jump distances of ten light-years, a normal flight would see the starship jump several times through interstellar space until it is about half a light-year out from its target star. It is in this phase where the most precise vector alignment is achieved, and considerable time is taken to ensure the track is correct. As fuel and time equals money, this is where a skillful captain can reduce costs by an appreciable margin. When the starship is lined up correctly, it will jump into the target planet's emergence zone.

Structure

All ZTT starships are spherical when jumping, although sensors and heat-dump panels are extended when flying between jump coordinates or in orbit. A starship's fusion generators, general systems, tanks, reaction drive, cargo bay, and crew modules are contained inside the lattice of jump nodes, which itself is covered by a hull of monobonded silicon.

Starship functions vary enormously, as does size. There are cargo ships, which form the majority of Confederation ships, warships, scoutships, cruise liners, colony vessels, private yachts, independent traders, astronomy research vessels, etc. And with over 500 star systems producing their own marques, all of these types have innumerable variants.

It is extremely difficult and expensive to provide a ground-to-orbit capability for a sphere which is primarily designed for deep-space operation, so many starships also carry atmospheric flyers. The only exception to this is warships, where cost and environmental concerns are not limiting factors, though the number of assault cruisers capable of planetary landings is very small. Certainly every Confederation planet prohibits the use of fusion drives inside the atmosphere; indeed most have a lower orbital altitude limit of 500km for fusion drive ships of any kind.

Fusion Drive

Legally, only fusion drives may be used within Confederation territory. He_3 and deuterium are available at every space port, and fusion provides a more than adequate performance for legitimate commercial and military operations. The amount of fuel used to power a jump is negligible in comparison to the delta-V requirement to match velocities with target star systems, and most commercial starships carry enough fuel reserves for five voyages. Reaction control is provided by hydrocarbon fluid similar to paraffin being pumped into the exhaust nozzles, where it is vaporized by electricity from the fusion generators.

Antimatter Drive

Possession of antimatter is a capital crime anywhere within the Confederation, and no other law is enforced so rigorously. Confederation Navy captains have the legal authority to execute any starship captain found carrying this substance in his or her ship. However, ships can legally be fitted with an antimatter drive, although moves are in progress in the Confederation Assembly to eliminate this final legal loophole. A small number do carry this system, mainly independent traders who will hire out as mercenaries to any government or institution wishing to wage covert war. The usual excuse by captains of such ships is that they bought their craft with the system already fitted, and its removal would cost too much.

An antimatter drive gives a starship a colossal delta-V reserve, and provides a high-gee maneuvering capability, typically in excess of 15 gees. The upper limit is dictated by the ship's structural capacity and the crew's endurance threshold (a cosmonik crew can withstand up to 20 gees for limited periods). It should be noted that a great many naval ships belonging to Confederation member states, even though not assigned to Confederation Navy squadrons, contain the necessary mountings, internal space, and control circuits for an antimatter drive, and all are stressed to withstand an acceleration exceeding that provided by their fusion drive.

Combat Wasps

These are hyper-gee attack missiles fired by starships (both ZTT and voidhawk or blackhawk) to engage their target. Starships are far too valuable to risk in direct assaults, although most have integral beam weapons as a final-layer defense against kinetic missiles. Combat wasps come in every size and function, including both attack and defense, and once launched they are fully autonomous. They carry a multitude of independent submunitions, including beam weapons (energy and particle), kinetic missiles, fusion bombs, decoy chaff, and electronic-warfare pods.

Also available are antimatter combat wasps providing a much greater performance than the fusion-powered versions. They are subject to the same proscription as antimatter.

Zero-Tau

Zero-tau is a method of stasis employed by most starships for their passengers. The system normally consists of a pod large enough to hold a human body, although anything can be stored inside it, and there is no theoretical limit as to how large such a unit can be, provided enough power is available to sustain it.

When activated, the pod surface is cloaked in a

midnight-black field effect, and the flow of time effectively halts within it. The contents of a zero-tau pod are also impervious to acceleration forces as the stasis locks the material inside into a specific space-time coordinate. This effect is utilized to full effect by starships fitted with antimatter drives. During combat they are capable of accelerating at well over 30 gees, which would crush a human body, even one augmented by nanonic supplements. So, for periods while the antimatter drive is on, the crew will go into zero-tau, allowing the flight computer to carry out a pre-programmed maneuver.

Most starship passengers prefer to use zero-tau than stay active during a flight. Any flight is extremely boring and, even with Confederation medical technology, free fall nausea is common. The most extensive zero-tau usage is in colony carrier starships, which typically carry 500 people at a time. The life-support requirements for so many active passengers would be prohibitively expensive to provide, and would more than double the size of the starship. Instead, zero-tau means that colonists can be carried in the same way as cargo, and also no on-board facilities are necessary for them. The only requirement for zero-tau is the large amount of power it consumes, which necessitates several fusion generators per craft.

Zero-tau is also the standard method of carrying animals on starships, although artificial hibernation is frequently used by colonists to stage-one worlds, principally because of the cost of a portable zero-tau pod.

Since zero-tau's development in 2121, as an adjunct

of ZTT physics, it has been employed regularly by people who wish to "time-travel" and see the future. The standard requirement for this is to establish a trust fund to pay for pod maintenance and power, then go into zero-tau for decades at a time. As such it tends to involve people who have a reasonable degree of wealth to begin with. Several extremely wealthy old people have gone into long-duration zero-tau after leaving instructions that they are to be brought out only when a full rejuvenation technology has been perfected.

Antimatter Planet-Busters

These are the weapons most feared across the Confederation. They are also the simplest to build once a source of antimatter has been established. Essentially, they need just a confinement chamber for a large amount of antimatter built into a missile capable of penetrating a planetary atmosphere. Typically, they are bombs in the multi-teraton range. Once detonated, their blast is sufficient to wreck an entire planetary climate, and saturate the surface with a lethal level of radioactive fallout. They take the old concept of nuclear winter one stage further—into nuclear hurricane. The amount of thermal energy pumped into an atmosphere will result in extremely high-speed storms raging for over a decade before they finally begin to dissipate.

Though the Black Syndicates are the producers of antimatter, little information is available about these shadowy organizations. They appear to be made up from people and organizations who have acquired a great deal of wealth by illegal means, typically armaments and proscribed stimulants. This money is needed to purchase the machinery required to produce antimatter on an industrial scale. As the majority of this equipment can have legitimate civil applications, its acquisition is relatively simple. For the core of the operation, all that is necessary is a few cargo starships and a crew of technicians to assemble and run the station. Typically, a station will be placed in orbit around a star just outside the Confederation's boundaries—and also far enough away to minimize discovery by navy patrols.

Cooperation and secrecy are enforced by customized neural nanonics, which are provided to everyone involved. They run specialist programs which monitor everything the user says. If the program determines that the user is being forced to divulge details of the operation, they will kill him. These neural nanonics cannot be circumvented or surgically removed, and once implanted they are there for life.

Four

Members of the Confederation in 2610

The Confederation includes 861 terracompatible planets settled by Adamist humans, 525 of them with a technoeconomy advanced enough to build starships, twelve xenoc planets, and three joint human-xenoc (Tyrathca) colony worlds. In addition to planets, there are 12,370 independent asteroid settlements (all Adamist), and five independent bitek habitats. The Edenists have germinated 8,310 bitek habitats, but colonized just one planet (Atlantis).

All their governments are represented in the Confederation Assembly on Avon, with voting rights proportionate to their population and development status.

Confederation territory in 2611 is a roughly spherical zone of space some 600 light-years in diameter, with Earth at its center. The main purpose of the Confederation is to guarantee free passage to all ships throughout this territory, and to prevent the use of weapons of mass destruction. To this end, all the numerous members pay a tax to the Confederation to finance its administration and its navy. A secondary function of the Confederation is to act as arbitrator in disputes and to establish a framework for unified interstellar law. More recently it has become involved in monitoring human rights violations on planets with oppressive constitutions or leaderships, an activity which does not have the wholehearted support of the entire Assembly.

The Confederation Navy

There are ten fleets, with a total fleet strength of 9,000 ZTT warships, and a further 2,000 auxiliaries, mainly concerned with communications and supply. Of the warships, 1,000 are dedicated starships, forming the core of each fleet, with crews made up from career personnel. The remainder of the fleet strength is composed of ship squadrons on assignment from national government navies, with a further 5,000 pledged should the Assembly declare an emergency situation. There are also a number of voidhawks on naval duty, typically 1,000 to 1,300 at any given time. Their captains traditionally sign on for a seven-year tour.

The Confederation Navy headquarters is an asteroid, Trafalgar, in orbit 110,000km above Avon. It serves variously as the main career officer academy, a repair and maintenance port, a Marine barracks, signals coordination center, and 1st Fleet base. It is also the premier research center for supralight communications, the so-called hyper-radio, with physicists from across the Confederation contributing to this project.

The First Admiral of the Fleet is Samuel Aleksandrovich, sixty-seven, appointed in 2605, a Confederation Navy career officer. All Confederation Navy fleets, and their individual squadrons, are always commanded by career officers who have renounced their national citizenship. Edenists are all given career officer status, as they can hardly renounce their culture. In peacetime, the navy's primary duty is to patrol and observe, with major exercises undertaken every four years. It is the Confederation Navy squadrons which are assigned to enforce sanction blockades (such as Omuta) ordered by the Assembly. And special reconnaissance craft (usually voidhawks) routinely examine both uninhabited stars within Confederation territory and stars around the fringe, searching for illegal antimatter stations.

In times of emergency, the navy's primary duty is to stop antagonists from attacking each other until a settlement can be reached by the Assembly arbitrators. The major problem with these emergencies, especially the small "bush fire" actions between independent asteroid settlements, is the speed at which they arise and are conducted, and the fact that governments always employ mercenary craft to avoid culpability. To counter this the navy has a large Intelligence operation watching for such flare-ups.

Confederation Navy Intelligence Service

Because of the conflicting loyalties which may arise during Confederation Navy service, Intelligence commissions are only available to career officers. It is the CNIS's job to correlate political data in the hope of predicting likely flare points. The sheer number of asteroid settlements precludes an officer being stationed on each one of them, so the service relies heavily on the larger national Intelligence services to keep an eye on neighboring governments. The CNIS does have a bureau on every member planet, however, down to stage-one colonies. Very few CNIS covert operations are launched against governments and institutions of industrialized worlds, and those that are must be personally approved by the First Admiral, who may find himself called before the Assembly to justify his reasons, not least to the government concerned.

The other major functions of the CNIS are to track down pirates and black syndicate antimatter stations. Again considerable cooperation with national Intelligence agencies is the norm in these instances, enabling them to track the industrial equipment essential to such illicit operations. The CNIS also possesses a large scientific division dedicated to monitoring weapons development, legal and otherwise, among Confederation member states and their corporations.

1. Sol System

Earth

Govcentral is responsible for civil administration on Earth, as well as the O'Neill Halo. It is a democracy, with separate continental congresses and a thousand-seat senate. However, barely 50 percent of the population bothers voting.

The planet suffered from vast ecological damage during the twenty-first century, culminating in the armada storms, while its population was estimated to reach in excess of 40,000,000,000 by 2160. Govcentral took drastic measures, including building the arcologies to protect the population from a lethal environment, spreading geneered tapegrass across the land surface as the remaining vegetation was destroyed, and seeding the oceans with an alga to act as a carbon sink. Newly discovered terracompatible worlds were employed purely as a method of disposing of the surplus population. Financial incentives to resettle were offered to the middle classes, while poor (welfare-dependent) districts were cleared out en masse. Towards the end of the Great Dispersal, 2250 saw upwards of 5,000,000 people being deported per week, in a fleet of 4,000 starships with a capacity of 5,000 passengers each.

Population is now officially stable at 38bn, though unofficial estimates place it closer to 42bn. Emigration has dropped to a steady 70,000,000 people per year, a figure which includes involuntary transportation. The penalty for virtually every crime, from rape to tax evasion, is now deportation. The entire population lives in arcologies, a term which has come to incorporate any urban area that has been covered against the weather.

In Asia, Africa and South America, the original city-in-a-building concept was employed on a massive scale, as didactic education and industrialization caught up with expanding population. There most arcologies consist of a vast metal gridwork, with pre-assembled factory-built housing modules, shops, offices, industrial units, etc., stacked into place and plugged into the utilities, all newly founded. Such giga-constructs are less common in Europe, Japan, and North America, where reorganization of existing cities and towns was the norm.

Each arcology produces its own food in factories and vats, the land being unfarmable, with the tapegrass coverage now total. Imported delicacies account for 30 percent of imports in revenue terms.

Government

Earth is now officially a republic with a single government, Govcentral. Consolidation of regional governments was a gradual process throughout the twenty-first century, aided considerably by the steady globalization of markets, uniform communication and data access, and the European federalist movement as well as other regional associations. With the introduction of fusion power, currency variations began to level out, effectively producing a uniform currency from 2075.

The various legal and administrative mechanisms for a global government were in place by the end of the twenty-first century, and the actual consolidation took place in 2103. At the time there was considerable resistance from nationalists across the globe; however, the worsening ecological crisis required a uniform response from the authorities. The arcologies were also established by this time, allowing for considerable regional autonomy while alleviating the fear of direct rule by "foreigners." Each arcology was so obviously independent that the loss of democratic accountability to some distant bureaucratic council wasn't a convincing argument against consolidation.

To begin with, Govcentral was pitched as being nothing more than a central international legal body and political congress, with a small police force. It soon evolved from this starting point to become a super-federalist state with the power of direct taxation (originally required to raise money for Earth's strategic-defense network). A security service was also established at that time, with extensive investigatory powers to help neutralize any remaining terrorist threat from die-hard nationalists. This has subsequently developed into the Govcentral Internal Security Directorate, which is charged with safeguarding the republic from all threats.

Each arcology has its own Parliament (and mayor) and each continent has its own assembly, both of which exert considerable authority; but they are all accountable to the Govcentral senate. A new president is elected directly every six years, and is responsible for setting the annual budget.

In reality, the entire structure is overbureaucratic and hopelessly inefficient. However, due to its monolithic size and the length of time it has now been in operation, any major change seems just about impossible.

Environment

The environmental damage caused throughout the twenty-first century by industrializing what was the "Third World" with cheap fusion power and advanced cybernetic production systems—so that everyone could enjoy a Western level of consumerism, medicine, and energy consumption—has left a catastrophic legacy. Although toxic pollution was tackled with a reasonable degree of success, the heat pollution produced by 38,000,000,000 people living in the comfort of a universal industrial civilization is now impossible to dispose of. Officially, Govcentral policy is to restore the planet's ecology to its pre-twenty-first-century state, but the sheer scale of the problem and the enormous potential cost means that the reclamation programs are chronically underfunded.

Despite all these problems, life for the population overall is very reasonable, certainly compared to the twentieth century. Didactic education has effectively eliminated illiteracy, while standards of living inside arcologies is comparable with many industrial planets, and is in fact slightly higher than the Confederation average. Unemployment is officially 9 percent, and crime is kept broadly under control by the police, with drug- and gang-related crimes the most common offenses.

Energy

Earth is totally dependent on clean fusion to provide power: the deuterium–He_3 reaction. Without a steady supply of He_3 from Jupiter, the fusion reactors would have to switch to less clean reactions such as deuterium–deuterium, producing a large waste-disposal problem. Whatever their source of fuel, the fusion plants simply cannot be switched off. The arcologies are the only habitable places on the planet, and they are totally technologically dependent. Govcentral has no way out of its reliance on the Edenists for provision of He_3, and has come to accept this situation. In turn the Edenists see themselves as morally bound to continue supplying the Earth, come what may. The Govcentral–Edenist political alliance is the strongest (and oldest) in the Confederation, and together they form the largest single voting block in the Assembly. As a result, the value of the commerce between Earth and Jupiter, on its own, exceeds the GDP of many industrialized planets.

Transport

The only links between the arcologies are the vac-train routes—tunnels maintained in a high vacuum, running magnetic levitation trains. Aircraft simply cannot operate in Earth's turbulent atmosphere, and the only surface vehicles left in operation are heavily armored transports used by ecology crews. Vac-trains provide a fast, ecologically sound transport system, with the trains reaching up to Mach 15 on some of the longer trans-Pacific routes. They were developed in tandem with the arcologies, and all the previous roads and surface-rail networks were allowed to decay.

Orbital Towers

One unique aspect of Earth is that surface-to-orbit spacecraft (spaceplanes or the newer ion-field flyers) have been banned. Again, heat pollution is the reason. While the contribution which hypersonic passenger aircraft fleets made to global warming remains debatable, the impact of 8,000 spaceplanes aerobraking into the atmosphere on a daily basis is not. Earth is therefore the only planet in the Confederation to have built orbital towers, starting in 2180 with the African tower. There are now five of them, handling all passenger and cargo traffic to and from the planet.

The O'Neill Halo

This is a ring of 974 asteroid settlements, in orbit (120,000km) above the Earth, with a population of 435m. Every settlement comes under the jurisdiction of Govcentral and has its own democratically elected council; the Halo has its own congress (the same as any continent) and forty-five representatives in the planetary senate. The first asteroids were funded by companies eager for new business ventures and the high profit levels resulting from microgravity manufacturing; and though über-capitalist culture still thrives, Halo corporate legislation is less restrictive than on Earth. This fact has helped to build the Halo into the largest concentration of non-Edenist manufacturing in the Confederation, with a technology equal to that of the Edenists and the Kulu Kingdom, producing 62 percent of Earth's export earnings. Now that many of the first asteroids are mined out, producing often three or four caverns per rock, the Halo settlements accommodate the largest asteroid populations to be found within the Confederation, with up to 400,000 people living in the largest.

The Halo Economy

Power for the asteroids comes from a mix of fusion and solar panels. Fusion tends to be used for the biosphere heating and lighting requirements, and for heavy industry, while solar panels are employed for the smaller (free-flying) industrial stations. Between 2125 and 2230, large starship assembly stations were built by Govcentral to provide Earth with its colony ships for the Great Dispersal, giving the Halo an early advantage in this field, which it has capitalized upon. Starships remain its premier export, and its maintenance, support, and refit industries are second to none. Contracts with the Govcentral Navy (the largest single defense procurement agency in the Confederation) form an essential financial pillar for the astroengineering companies, which allows them to tender extremely competitive prices.

The Sol system's location at the center of the Confederation, Earth's vast consumer markets, the starship industry, trade with Jupiter, the asteroid belt, Luna, and Mars, all contribute to making the Halo the second greatest spaceport in the Confederation (after Jupiter), with 12,000 starship movements daily. Halo citizens enjoy a much higher standard of living than their cousins on Earth.

Independent Asteroid Settlements

There are 1,820 independent asteroid settlements in the Sol system: 1,485 in the main belt, 183 in the Jovian Trojan points, 137 in the Apollo Amour asteroids, 3 in the Oort cloud, and the remaining 12 distributed across the outer system. Total population is estimated to be 1,200,000,000. Most of these settlements are fiercely independent. Since 2150 they have been founded by Halo inhabitants who wanted to break free of Govcentral restrictions, groups from Belt settlements which became overpopulated, and various other breakaway movements.

As with the Confederation as a whole, just about every ideology and religion can be found among the settlements. The Belt Alliance is the unifying government, although it is a very loose union, and non-political, with 764 actual members and most of the others affiliated. It is the Belt Alliance that provides the representation for settlement citizens in the Confederation Assembly. The main function of the Belt Alliance is to fund and maintain a naval force which contributes to the overall defense of the solar system.

The Moon–Mars Partnership

This constitutes a separate, and unique, political entity outside Govcentral's sphere of control.

History

Mars is the only planet in the Confederation to be terraformed. With the development of the ZTT drive, and now an abundance of "standard" terracompatible planets, the entire Mars project is a historical aberration which will probably never be repeated. The project's origin can be traced directly back to the establishment in 2020 of the first Lunar industrial base.

The Clavius moonbase venture was intended to mine and develop the substantial quantity of sub-crystal ice and other volatiles (mainly nitrates) which had been located around the Moon's poles. It was the first ever large-scale commercial (i.e. non-governmental) space project, and its importance in the subsequent development of human space exploration cannot be understated.

Initially it was intended that the Lunar icefields should supply the newly established, and proliferating, low-Earth orbit (LEO) microgee factories and their dormitory modules with water and other chemicals at a much cheaper rate than lifting them from Earth. This initial premise was met swiftly enough, and the parent companies rapidly expanded the operation to supply reaction-mass fuel (hydrogen) to inter-orbit spacecraft, and soon after (2030) to the first interplanetary ships. As a result, Clavius was expanded and another three bases, Zach, Schiller, and Plato, were established.

The first asteroid-capture mission (of a stony-iron rock) in 2040 was a critical point in the future of the Lunar bases; their parent companies bid for the asteroid's biosphere contract. Given the prodigious quantity of water and nitrogen and carbon required for even a modest biosphere, the only alternative was a dual-capture mission, with a carbonaceous chondritic asteroid as well as the stony-iron one being brought into Earth orbit. So naturally the moonbases won the contract, and immediately began scaling up their operations by a factor of twenty.

Even before the first asteroid arrived in Earth orbit in 2047 three more capture missions were launched by new consortiums. Jupiter flights were in preparation, and proposals for possible asteroid belt settlements were under consideration. Mining output from the Moon rose from about 10,000 tons a year in 2040 to over 500,000 tons by 2050. Then it tripled again in the next twenty years.

By 2045 it was obvious that the moonbases were going to be permanent; far from reducing the Moon's importance, as many finance analysts had predicted, the arrival of the asteroids in Earth orbit was going to enhance the Moon's economic and financial status considerably. Plans for more substantial habitation complexes were drawn up and implemented. Until this time the mining bases were little more than company camps, equivalent to the twentieth century's oil-rig platforms. Now, though, underground cities were bored out under the regolith, powered by fusion generators.

What was at that time the most ambitious geneering project to date was undertaken to adapt the children of the Moon's inhabitants to the low gravity field. Calcium-production rate was increased, and muscles in general and heart muscles in particular were strengthened against atrophy. Such adaptations were reasonably successful: certainly the first children to be born with them lived to an age comparable to their equivalents born on Earth at the same time. Subsequent improvements enhanced life expectancy considerably.

The Moon's population is now 100 percent the product of geneering, a program of modification second only to the Edenists. Unfortunately, although its people are perfectly adapted to their low-gravity environment, they are uncomfortable in higher gravity. Unless gestated in a one-gravity field, adaptation is a very long and arduous process. Though their muscles and bones don't waste away, they are not strong enough initially to withstand the higher gravity field for long periods of time— a fact which came to play a major part in the decision to terraform Mars.

Over the next thirty years another fifteen cities were established, making a total of twenty-two, with the Lunar population increasing to 1.5m. Full civil independence was granted to the city settlements in 2055, and the Moon was admitted to the UN Assembly the following year. Following its elevation to nationhood, a local Parliament was formed, which began to formulate long-term policies. Until this time the Moon was virtually a one-industry territory. This helped facilitate an inter-city (effectively an inter-company) pricing arrangement, so that bulk chemical exports were universally priced. Moon material was marketed and distributed through a single organization, the Lunar Export Board (LEB). Mining machinery and launch systems were also standardized. Such collective arrangements contributed greatly to the sense of community which led to the subsequent social development of the new nation.

The most important priority of the new Parliament was to diversify the Moon's economy away from mining. Such manufacturing systems as there were at that time tended to concentrate on equipment needed for the mining operations, and for the larger machinery used to bore out and maintain the big city chambers. Technology research programs were started, and companies were given advantageous start-up packages. Ten percent of the revenue from the LEB was allocated to developing new industries appropriate to the lunar environment. This objective proved a difficult task, because competition from the O'Neill Halo for markets was tough, and the Halo had the advantage of microgee facilities as well as offering its workers a full-gravity environment when they came off shift. But with continuing investment from the LEB, and an expanding highly educated workforce, a great deal of progress was made towards complete technical autonomy.

2090 proved to be a turning point for the Moon, just as much as for the Eden habitat. In both cases the Moon's mineral and chemical exports were 2m tons a year, and a small market for manufactured goods had been established. The O'Neill Halo had seventeen asteroids, with another eight on their way to Earth, and still more planned. However, with regular supplies of He_3 arriving from Jupiter, and its price about to go down with the advent of the first operational cloudscoop, fusion was becoming extremely cheap and widely available. It was looking obvious that a carbonaceous chondritic asteroid-capture mission was now a practical proposition (nuclear explosives couldn't be used, since a carbonaceous chondritic asteroid didn't have the tensile strength to withstand the shock wave; instead a continuous thrust engine of some kind had to be attached which would slowly maneuver the asteroid into its new orbit).

The Lunar Parliament advanced two far-reaching proposals which were put to the entire population for a referendum:

1. Now that fusion will, in the near future, effectively end our monopoly of supplying water, carbon, and nitrogen to the O'Neill Halo, we advocate that the LED fund a carbonaceous chondritic asteroid-capture mission in order to retain its traditional business of supplying these chemicals to the Halo. Public ownership of the LEB shall be formalized, making every citizen a shareholder, so that all future profits accrued from its ventures may be distributed equitably. The Government shall retain two-thirds of the equity, and remain in charge of policy.

2. With the advent of such a mission closing down our indigenous mines, we must determine new goals for ourselves and our descendants. Clearly our physiology prevents us from returning en masse to Earth; and even the Halo asteroids in their present configuration offer limited habitation prospects. As we do not, under any circumstances, contemplate fostering our un-

born children to another culture and then simply withering away ourselves, we advance two options for your consideration. The first is to capture a stony-iron asteroid and place it in the Halo. This asteroid will have a standard biosphere, but will be spun up to a rate which provides a lunar gravity level on the cavern floor. This will allow us to transfer all our industrial capacity to the Halo, and abandon the Moon. Thereafter we will become a fully fledged Halo nation, able to expand our domain accordingly. The second option is of an extremely long-term nature: the terraforming of Mars. Owing to the sheer size of this goal, commitment to achieving it will have to be total, which in practice will require a vote in excess of 70 percent. We estimate that one-third of our resources will have to be dedicated to that project over a period no shorter than five hundred years. No other conceivable goal would be as hard to realize, nor as rewarding to succeed. The result will be an entire planet uniquely suitable to our descendants.

After these propositions were made, one month was allocated for public debate. During that same month, Eden declared independence, and launched its buyout of the JSKP.

In all probability, it was Eden's declaration of independence, or more likely the response from Earth, which settled the debate for the Lunar electorate. The

Unified Christian Church promptly excommunicated the Edenists, and the JSKP board launched a legal battle against the buyout which took seventeen years to resolve (in Eden's favor).

Because of their large sense of community, amplified by the way they cooperated in promoting their single major industry, and their physiological diversity from "Earth humans," the Lunar cities chose the Mars option.

It has subsequently been argued, with some justification, that the Lunar citizens didn't so much choose Mars as reject the O'Neill Halo. At that time, and to this day, the Halo was dedicated to the capitalist ethic, financial conflict and competition being the principal basis of its culture. And its reaction to Eden's attempt to buy out the JSKP was hostile in the extreme (understandable given that so many of the Halo's own companies were partners in the JSKP). The Moon, with its gentler and more cooperative spirit, was uneasy about joining with such a culture, preferring a more noble, humanistic approach to life; although physical separation from the majority of the Halo would have been maintained due to the different gravity environment they required, that multicommercial arena was the one they would have been thrown headlong into, and in all probability they would have been assimilated and destroyed inside it.

Whatever their psychological reasoning, they voted instead to terraform Mars, with 78 percent in favor, 7 percent opposed, and the remaining 15 percent either don't knows or abstaining.

As a result of this vote, Parliament immediately authorized two carbonaceous chondritic asteroid-capture missions. The national Lunar industrial steering committee had decided that their economic strength lay in their very size, a unified nation being a difficult force to reckon with. And they determined to use their wealth, such as it was, to retain their monopoly on supplying of water and nitrates to the O'Neill Halo for as long as possible.

The Moon's subsequent switch to a pure Communist economy, and philosophy, is usually considered to be a result of this decision, although some political analysts maintain that the Lunar cities simply developed into the ultimate corporate state.

Pursuing this strength-through-size policy, Parliament began to nationalize the industrial facilities of every Lunar city over the next decade. By 2100 the Moon was effectively a Communist world, with every major economic asset owned by the State Industrial Institute (SII), and every member of the populace owning a voting share in the Institute. The SII was set up with a charter decreeing that a full third of its profits were to be used to fund the Mars terraforming project. That aside, it acted like a very large capitalist corporation competing in many commercial arenas. Most notably these were low-density structures, and micro-function supermolecules (the latter researched for their use in the terraforming project, and the precursor of today's programmable silicon); but the LEB also managed to retain its monopoly on supplying the O'Neill Halo with water and nitrates until 2180, and even today it remains their largest single supplier.

Unlike the earlier Communist regimes of the twentieth century, noted principally for their brutality and totalitarianism, the Lunar government is a very benign culture. It is probably true to say that this is only possible due to the Lunar Constitution, which was enacted by a People's Congress (itself electronic), held in 2096–7, that enfranchised every citizen with an electronic vote in every major parliamentary issue (curiously, in the current constitution the only proposition excluded from a total vote is one aimed at terminating the Mars project). The constitution decrees that a Parliament acts as the national executive, with a five-yearly Electronic General Congress (in which every citizen has a vote) as the ultimate national authority; it also allows for administrative power to be diversified to Mars as that planet's population increases and the Moon's population declines. Public freedom of information and a very rigorous civil-service watchdog agency, accountable only to the General Congress and not to Parliament, mean that the opportunities for mischief and personal aggrandizement so prevalent among earlier Communist politicians by and large no longer exist.

With both the economic and political mechanism in place, the terraforming officially began in 2103. All contracts issued by the Terraforming Office are taken up by Lunar companies, with subcontracting to outside companies kept to an absolute minimum.

Mars Terraforming: Timetable of Events

2091   Terraforming Office formed to oversee the entire project. Strategy formulation begins.

2103   Thoth base established on Mars, and industrial stations assembled at Phobos.

2105   Major geological survey instituted.

2106   Small (2km diameter) carbonaceous chondritic asteroid arrives at Phobos to provide raw material for biological refinery stations. Over the next four centuries sixty-five carbonaceous chondritic asteroids are consumed by the Phobos stations.

2108   Phobos biological refinery stations produce a genetically modified microbe to liberate oxygen from soil and rock, and begin seeding it into the planet's atmosphere. Production is continuous.

2125   First carbonaceous chondritic impact mission started. The asteroid, named Braun, measures 15km in diameter.

2126   Start of comprehensive asteroid and Oort belt survey to locate large ice asteroids (20km+ diameter).

2139   Braun impacts on Mars equator, with colossal gas and energy release. Atmosphere completely saturated with particles, and average temperature raised 0.7° Celsius.

2140   Second carbonaceous chondritic impact mission started: Oberth.

2145   A microbe which produces chlorofluorocarbons (greenhouse gases) from soil salts is seeded by Phobos. Production is continuous.

2152   Oberth impact.

2153–2320 Twenty-two large carbonaceous chondritic asteroid impact missions.

2180 Carbon dioxide ice caps dissolve completely.

2200 Surface pressure 35 millibars.

2235 Photoactive longchain supermolecule (Artificial Life) produced by Phobos stations to extract nitrogen from subsurface nitrate deposits. Seeding begins.

2300 Surface pressure 80 millibars.

2310 First ice asteroid impact mission.

2310–2500 Forty ice asteroid impact missions.

2350 Improved nitrogen-extracting supermolecules produced at Phobos.

2360 First free water found in deep depressions.

2370 Slowlife introduced, being geneered organisms capable of functioning in a low-energy environment: lichens, worms, algae, and aquatic mollusks. Their primary function is to digest atmospheric carbon dioxide.

2390 Rain falls on Olympus Mons.

2400 Surface pressure 200 millibars.

2425 New phase of geneering to Lunar children, giving them enhanced lung capacity ready for Mars environment.

2460 Thoth city releases primary biota organisms into environment: hardy grasses, aquatic plants, fish, insects.

2500 Surface pressure 350 millibars. Average temperature 6° Celsius.

2510 Phobos biological refinery stations now given over entirely to extensive production of geneered bacteria to digest the remaining atmospheric carbon dioxide. Production of nitrogen-extracting long-chain supermolecules remains constant.

2512 Thoth city begins introduction of final ecology: high-order plants and animals.

2550 Surface pressure now 423 millibars, average temperature 11° Celsius. Mars officially declared habitable by Terraforming Office.

Subsequent History

Since the planet was made habitable, the originally expected exodus of the Moon's indigenous population to Mars hasn't happened. Although technically remaining one nation, there has been a perceptible sociocultural split between the two separate populations. The Lunar city inhabitants remain what can only be described as "cosmopolitan," preferring the cultural heritage of their five-hundred-year-old cities to the more basic amenities of Mars. (Of course, were they transferred en masse to Mars then their culture would go with them, but such an enforced move would be contrary to their constitution. The only two times this was proposed in the General Congress, it was voted down by a large margin.) But, nonetheless, the population drift to Mars is continual, albeit small, and consists mainly of the younger Lunar citizens. At the current rate it will be another two centuries before the Lunar population is depleted to such a level that sustaining its highly artificial and technology-dependent cities becomes impractical.

The most often cited reason for this reluctance to

transfer is the somewhat uncertain future they face on Mars. Although this may sound completely paradoxical given the awesome nature of their accomplishment in manufacturing an entire world's ecology, it is nevertheless a highly relevant observation. The total population base available to colonize Mars is only 6,000,000, which is extremely limiting. Just over 2,000,000 citizens remain on the Moon, 500,000 live in Phobos and Deimos, and the remaining 3,500,000 live on Mars itself, making it the most sparsely populated planet in the Confederation, bar stage-one colony worlds. Between them, this 6,000,000 can hardly develop the two planets' economy along standard colony lines even if they abandon their commitment to Communism and let capitalistic growth run unchecked: they simply do not have the numbers to proliferate the way other colony worlds do during their first century of existence.

The easy option would be to open Mars to immigration. However, there are factors operating against this. Firstly, their ancestors dedicated five centuries of effort specifically so that their descendants could have their own habitable low-gravity world. Allowing an influx of outsiders at this time would be a betrayal of their forefathers' trust on an inconceivable scale. Secondly, such an influx would inevitably destroy the entire nature of their chosen society. The Moon and Mars are virtually the only Confederation societies practicing pure Communism, and though it has served them extraordinarily well (indeed it is doubtful whether any other political ideology could have accomplished the terraforming of Mars), it is questionable that anyone not brought up in such a political environment from birth would be able to tolerate its doctrines. To outsiders, especially Earth dwellers (from whom any immigrant population would derive), they seem terribly restrictive. Indeed, there is already a growing trend among the youth born on Mars to question the traditional nature of their society. A disturbing number even appear to be almost rejecting the very inheritance of supertechnology which built their world, as well as the political heritage which made such a monumental task possible, and they are turning instead to a more primitive/spiritual philosophy.

The only conceivable way out of their current population dilemma would be to adopt a huge exowomb breeding program. There is a historical precedent in the Edenist culture, which used such a program to expand its population in the early years, and does still use exowombs quite extensively. Although this option has yet to be put before the General Congress, it is doubtful that it would be approved in the foreseeable future.

Physical Parameters of Mars
The Terraforming Office was renamed the Martian Bureau of Ecology in 2550, and was subsequently made responsible for reducing the carbon dioxide level to the optimum level of 1 percent, from that of 3.7 percent in 2610. This goal is predicted to be reached in 2630.

Vigorous planting schemes are in progress to reach this target, foresting vast areas with a variety of trees from right across the Confederation—the only world to follow such a policy. As there was no aboriginal ecology to disturb, such a mixture of plants was deemed acceptable, and desirable. Most Confederation worlds maintain a policy of minimal botanical contamination, with the exception of terrestrial food crops. Extensive prairie planting is also in hand on Mars. It is estimated that 70 percent of the land area has now been covered with high-order plants including mosses. The remaining 30 percent provides home to the older "primary biota," and even some surviving slowlife organisms. There have recently been two proposals in the Martian Parliament that some of these areas should be declared National Preservation Parks, and be left in their original state. Both times these proposals were turned down, but only by a small majority.

There are no continents, as such, on the planet. Despite the forty ice-asteroid impacts, and the unfrozen polar ice, water is not an abundant substance in comparison to other terracompatible worlds. Seas form in craters as well as in natural lower levels. However, the equatorial zone, having been subject to a total of sixty-five asteroid impacts, is now an almost continual band of sea, with only a few narrow strips of marshy land preventing it from becoming a complete circle of water. Salinity is generally very low, with some of the crater formations being essentially fresh-water seas.

There is very little seasonal variation in the weather. The equatorial zones are temperate, with the higher latitudes possessing a climate equivalent to Scandinavian countries. The polar circles are defined as anything above latitude 50°.

Terrestrial crops such as wheat, potatoes, maize, oats, and barley are grown by the collective farms. Up to three harvests per (Martian) year are the norm. The fishing industry is well developed, a large number of different species having been introduced into the seas.

Physiology

Lunar and Martian inhabitants have all been geneered to a common design criterion, although the current physique was arrived at in two distinct phases. The first round of adaptations was begun in 2030, so that the Lunar city dwellers could live in a low-gravity environment. Some subtle modifications were made to their glands to offset the atrophy imbalances which occur from prolonged exposure to the Moon's gravity. To prevent calcium depletion, their bones were made thicker than an average human's, and they tend to be more thickly muscled, again to prevent wasting.

The second phase was initiated in 2425, when it became clear that the Martian atmosphere was not going to be of a terracompatible standard immediately after terraforming was complete, since there was an excessive amount of carbon dioxide, and the nitrogen ratio was well below norm. Therefore lung capacity was increased by 40 percent, which required some general enlargement of the ribcage and upper torso as well as expanding heart size to cope with the increased quantity of blood vessels in the bigger lungs. Combined with the earlier modifications, Lunar and Martian citizens now uniformly appear stocky and broad-shouldered with prominent chests, although most are actually of above-average height.

Although they can tolerate high gravity, prolonged

exposure to it is tiring for them unless they have already spent over a year adapting. Inevitably, all their starship crews possess nanonic supplements, and their ships do not generally accelerate above 1.5 gees.

Economy

As mentioned above, the SII is run along lines similar to an ordinary commercial conglomerate. It owns shares in every industrial enterprise on the Moon and on Mars: these vary from large factories, which are owned in conjunction with local councils, to collective farms, and cooperative companies. Even individual (single-person) businesses, such as software-writing or design, are run in conjunction with the SII. And, in addition to the Lunar and Martian companies, it owns an extensive range of commercial enterprises across the Sol system and beyond: in manufacturing, raw material, refining, communication, and transport industries.

With the exception of the Edenist helium-mining operation, the SII is possibly the largest commercial concern in the Sol system. The largest and most important industries it administers are the LEB, which supplies water and other chemicals to the O'Neill Halo, and the factories which produce programmable silicone, in which the SII is the acknowledged market leader.

Interestingly, for a company run entirely by committed Communists, the SII is a ruthless competitor in both its local system and the interstellar markets. As it once had the unenviable task of making enough profit annually to fund the terraforming operation, it could never afford to be anything else than 100 percent efficient.

But, now that the terraforming is essentially over, and only a fraction of the old Terraforming Office's budget is required by the Martian Bureau of Ecology, a much larger amount of funding is available for industrial and social investment. The effect this has had during the last fifty years is quite obvious: the SII has expanded both its size and market share by over 4 percent annually, while economic growth rate in the solar system has remained around the 1 percent level for centuries. Both Lunar and Martian standards of living have risen accordingly. Although collectively wealthy, for the last 500 years their populations have endured a socioeconomic index which was the lowest in the solar system generally, purely because of the sacrifices necessary to pay for the Mars terraforming project.

Now, though, with more hard currency available, they are becoming an important market for domestic consumer products. (The SII itself tends to concentrate on heavy-industry enterprises.) Import businesses are booming here, and foreign-brand goods are becoming quite a status symbol, particularly among the young.

Defense

The government must pay an annual contribution for the upkeep of the Confederation Navy. Thanks to various cooperative treaties, the Moon is part of the Govcentral strategic-defense network, to which it contributes financially, and many SII-owned industrial stations work on defense manufacturing subcontracts. The Strategic Defense zone extends out to 2.5m km from Earth, and sensor coverage of it is absolute. Any starship which does not emerge within the designated zones will be intercepted in an average time of fifteen seconds.

The number of interplanetary ships carrying commercial cargoes between Earth, the Halo, Belt Alliance settlements, Jupiter, Saturn, and Mars, is also the largest number operating in any solar system. Govcentral, Jupiter, the Belt Alliance and the Lunar nation have formed a defense association which monitors all system-wide traffic for any instance of piracy. Such a concentration of warships and patrol voidhawks makes the Sol system the safest place to travel inside the Confederation.

However, Mars, with its small population and relatively low economic output (for an entire planet), has little in the way of defense capability. A standard starship emergence detector sensor satellite network is in existence, although the coverage only extends out to 250,000km. Both Phobos and Demos are protected by weapons platforms. Thoth city has laser defenses against atmospheric-penetration missiles.

Because its citizens' physiology prohibits them from engaging in high-gee combat maneuvers, the Martian Lunar nation has no naval ships, although some of the SII's commercial starships have a secondary combat role in times of national emergency, and are capable of deploying combat wasps. A training exercise is held for them every ten years, though they have never seen active service.

2. Kulu

Kulu is an ethnic Christian terracompatible planet 173 light-years from Earth, discovered in 2227.

Physical Data

Kulu orbits 152m km from its star, giving it a 379-day year. Rotation takes 24 hours 8 minutes, gravity is 97 percent standard. Its axial tilt is 1.5°, giving moderate seasonal climate change.

Two-fifths of the surface area of Kulu is land, distributed among nine major continents and several archipelagos. Kulu has no polar continents, only ice caps. There are four major oceans.

It has two moons: Quorn is 1,500km in diameter, and orbits 100,000km out, giving each orbit a nine-day period. St. Mary is 2,300km in diameter, and orbits 490,000km out, giving it a six-week orbit. Both moons possess naval bases, and the Kulu Corporation has a mining operation on St. Mary.

One hundred and seventy-five stony-iron asteroids have been maneuvered into orbit 150,000km above Kulu, forming a large zero-gee industrial base. Their combined population is 18.5m.

Kulu's capital city is Nova Kong, sited on the east coast of the Althalia continent (the largest), 42° north of the equator, with a population of 19m. The planetary population is 3.75bn, making this the second most heavily populated planet after Earth. Emigration to the planet itself is now closed, though the asteroid settlements remain open to specialists.

Star System Physical Data

The Kulu system has five solid planets, including Kulu itself. The other four are:

	Meython	Octoberon	Ulvern	Bellrit
Orbital distance from star (million km)	23	73	178	250
Diameter (km)	5,600	4,900	15,850	8,000
Atmosphere	—		thin carbon dioxide/oxygen	weak carbon dioxide envelope
Atmospheric pressure				
Moons	1	—	2	1

There is a thin asteroid belt between Ulvern and Bellrit, comprised mainly of stony-iron rocks. A much larger belt orbits outside Bellrit, and supports 242 settlements. Their population is 50,000,000m.

There are also three gas giants.

	Tarron	Raverly	Gerrant
Orbital distance from star (million km)	760	1,100	2,900
Diameter (km)	150,000	115,000	103,000
Moons	27	15	9

The Kulu Kingdom

The Kulu Kingdom is composed of the capital planet, Kulu itself, and the principality planets (in order of discovery) Jerez, St. Albans, Nesko, Balurghat, Echtern, Warwick, Shasta, and Obmey. The nine member stars occupy a roughly ovoid shape fifty-seven light-years long, with Kulu itself the closest to Earth and Ombey furthest away. Its Royal Navy scoutships are still searching for new terracompatible planets; however, the cost of funding the Shasta and Ombey principalities precludes another colonization project being launched for another fifty years.

History

Kulu was settled in 2230 by Richard Saldana, the chairman of the New Kong company (an asteroid settlement in Earth's O'Neill Halo), who transported all the settlement's industrial stations to an asteroid in orbit around Kulu, and claimed the star system for himself. His reason for moving (or escape, as he called it), was to liberate the New Kong company from what he saw as the unnecessarily restrictive influence of Govcentral, as well as its equally anti-capitalistic tax regime.

Saldana was himself of European aristocratic background, with proven ancestral links to the British, Spanish and Greek royal families, a pedigree which undoubtedly helped his family in their later elevation to sovereign status. Although moving the New Kong industrial stations out of Halo jurisdiction was an act of dubious legality, Govcentral chose not to pursue Saldana. A naval action would probably only have succeeded in damaging or destroying the stations, and invading what was ostensibly an independent star system would have been politically disastrous at a time when Govcentral desperately needed unlimited access to colony planets in order to dump Earth's surplus population. Saldana's venture had been meticulously planned over several decades (he was eighty-seven when it happened), and considerable effort had gone into filling New Kong with people dissatisfied by both Govcentral and the alternatives offered by the colony planets, the majority of which at that time were extremely primitive.

Perhaps the most notorious decision he took was to prohibit the Edenists from germinating a habitat in orbit around Kulu's gas giant Tarron, and setting up their usual He_3 mining operation. He did this under the guise of religious devotion, although he had never before in his life demonstrated any religious tendencies. It is arguable that he was himself considering the establishment of an He_3 mining corporation to rival the Edenists, though Kulu at that time could never afford to match what was already the largest industrial enterprise in existence, and Saldana must have known this. Whatever the true reason, the Kulu Kingdom remains completely independent of the Edenists for its supplies of He_3 (see Gas giants, page 17).

With extensive modern manufacturing systems available in orbit around Kulu, Saldana was quickly able to provide a sophisticated infrastructure on the planet itself, attracting the kind of middle-class professionals who would otherwise have remained on Earth. With its

burgeoning economy, Kulu was swiftly recognized as
an excellent investment, and capital poured in—with
many of the wealthier individual investors following it,
raising its appeal still further. The economic upward
spiral of Kulu's first century is one that has never been
repeated, despite innumerable attempts; the economic
and social factors both on Earth and across the Confederation have changed too much since then. Richard Saldana was simply the right man at the right time with the
right idea.

Richard Saldana died in 2248, and his son Gerrald
inherited what had become the Kulu Corporation, which
then consisted of the asteroid settlement and its associated orbital industrial stations, the Tarron cloudscoop
operation, planetary utility services, a starship fleet, and
various planetary factories. In a move no less inspired
than his father's, Gerrald called the settlement's first
election, but refused to stand for any post. Instead it was
a simple matter to insure that his placemen secured a
majority in the Parliament, and the first action of the
new president, Dennis Mason (later Lord Mason), was
to introduce an act creating the position of a constitutional guardian who would remain outside politics and
safeguard the Kulu system's new-found liberty. The logical choice for this post was someone who simply could
not be bribed, so Gerrald Saldana's appointment was
approved unanimously by Parliament, and his coronation was held in 2250.

Constitution

The head of state is the King, who has the right to levy taxes in defense of the Kingdom, and is responsible for enforcing the Crown's justice. In return for fealty, the sovereign guarantees all his subjects the following rights: (a) an elected assembly which can offer advice to the Crown, pass laws subject to the royal seal of assent, and raise taxes to pay for the said laws; (b) an independent judiciary and police force not subject to Parliament's control; (c) the right to own and use property (widely referred to as the Capitalism Pledge, necessary to placate investors and wealthy would-be colonists becoming nervous that Gerrald was establishing a dictatorship).

Religion

The sovereign is also the defender of the Christian faith throughout the Kingdom, a position which wasn't ratified by the Vatican until 2343. Although atheists are allowed to immigrate, the devout of all other faiths are refused entry. King Marcus granted considerable estates to the Church in 2312, which have provided the synod with an independent income ever since. Kulu priests are frequently assigned to Christianizing missions on recently colonized planets.

The Monarchy

Gerrald Saldana took his duties as head of state very seriously, virtually handing over management of the Kulu Corporation to his son and daughter, Alastair and Cheloe, so that he could devote his energies to proper government. He established a socialized health service and several universities, as well as overseeing the formation of a genuinely independent judiciary. In short, he did effectively perform his role as constitutional guardian, cementing his family's power base. His greatest challenge came over the annexation of Jerez, which was discovered by Kulu Corporation ships but was also claimed by the Parma government. Up until that point, no government's jurisdiction had extended outside its own system (apart from the Edenists'). As usual in times of national crisis, the population rallied round its leader and, with Cheloe serving on one of the starships which fought the Parma ships attacking the Tarron cloudscoop, the Saldana dynasty became unchallengeable in Kulu from this period onwards. Parma was defeated with the use of antimatter weapons, its remaining industrial stations being confiscated in reparation, and Jerez became a principality awarded to Cheloe herself.

Since Gerrald's coronation, the greatest threat to the stability of the monarchy occurred during the abdication crisis of 2432 (see Tranquillity, page 127). However, the subsequent reign of King Lukas did much to repair the damage; he worked hard at eliminating the excesses of court corruption (which by then was becoming dangerously decadent), and along with Queen Anne enjoyed an extraordinarily high level of public popularity and support.

The Saldana Family
The King still owns the Kulu Corporation in its entirety (as well as possessing the mineral rights of all planets

and asteroids in the Kingdom), and because of this he is the richest individual in the whole Confederation today. The Kulu Corporation has expanded its interests to include manufacturing of every kind, and owns all the utilities on the capital planet and on each principality world. Also it administers the Crown Estates, which account for 80 percent of the land mass on each terracompatible planet, and it mines and supplies He_3 in each Kingdom system. The Kulu Crown Bank, a Kulu Corporation subsidiary, is the largest financial institution in the Kingdom, and contends with the Jovian Bank for business throughout the Confederation. It is the junior members of the Saldana family who run the corporation, with the sovereign's tenth sibling (see Saldana Eugenics, below) as its president. A spell of commissioned service in the Royal Navy is virtually compulsory for a Saldana, certainly for one belonging to the upper echelon, i.e. destined for public life. They normally serve a fifteen-year commission, although some go on to make a career out of it. For them promotion is always through merit, and several also hold high-ranking posts in the Confederation Navy (again earned on merit).

There are probably as many as 350,000 direct descendants of Richard Saldana alive today, three-quarters of whom are illegitimate. The Saldanas clearly enjoy their pre-eminent position, and its associated privileges, but rarely abuse it. Although all upper-echelon family members are expected to marry, fathering children outside their official marriages is not considered an abuse of privilege (rather a consequence), and the family invariably pays a generous allowance to the child's mother (King Aaron allegedly sired 409 offspring).

The escapades of the junior family members provide a constant source of amusement and gossip for the entire Kingdom's population, and indeed across the Confederation as a whole.

Saldana Eugenics and Hierarchy

Over the years, the Saldana family has received considerable genetic modification, improving the efficiency of both brain and body, and this process continues. They are physically impressive in size and vigor, although most of them possess a rather thin nose with a slight downward curve at the tip, which has become their (in)famous distinguishing mark, and their life expectancy is currently 180 plus. It's a common saying that Saldanas are like Edenists without the affinity gene.

All senior Saldanas undertake marriage, thus providing an ideal example of the Christian family to the general public. The first ten offspring of the King and Queen are grown in exowombs, and the eldest child (always male) eventually becomes King of Kulu, with the next eight assuming the thrones of the principality worlds (three princesses are the norm), while the tenth child becomes President of the Kulu Corporation. This same pattern is followed through every generation, which allows further genetic modifications to be made to the zygotes. After the tenth exowomb child has been birthed, the King and Queen (usually still Crown Prince and Princess at the time) are then free to conceive natural children. The usual number of these subsequent offspring is three or four, who act as a reserve in case any of the exowomb ten should be killed before assuming their allotted station in life.

The Crown Princess is always a subject of the Kulu Kingdom, and usually a member of the aristocracy. A family which has itself undergone extensive genetic modification (especially regarding life expectancy) is preferred, so that a long-term marriage partnership will be possible. The King and Queen can never get divorced, but it would be wrong to conclude that all royal marriages arranged by the court are arid couplings, and therefore loveless. Most significantly, King Lukas is reputed to have only ever enjoyed his partner, Queen Anne, as a sexual partner.

The Kings of Kulu

Gerrald	2250–2280
Alastair	2280–2302
Marcus	2302–2351
Aubrey	2351–2372
Aaron	2372–2412
James	2412–2432
Michael	2432 (abdicated before coronation)
Lukas	2432–2505
David	2505–2608
Alastair II	2608–

Kulu Aristocracy

Gerrald Saldana instigated a titled nobility the year following his coronation, thus formalizing the institution of monarchy. Letters patent of nobility were (and are) used as a reward for loyalty or public service (the highest carrying pensions and sometimes small estates), and in form it duplicates the original European system of ennoblement. The aristocracy do not sit in the equivalent of a House of Lords, but a great many of them work for the royal court in administering the sovereign's privileges, such as the granting of mineral-extraction licenses, the levying of taxes for defense, and as officers of justice, etc.—in effect, forming a private civil service unaccountable to Parliament. It is this court which runs Kulu's Intelligence services, and this is perhaps its most notorious function.

Technology
Kulu technology is second only to that of the Edenists, and in some fields, notably nanonics, it is more advanced. The capital system has a highly developed technoeconomy, providing its population with the best Adamist standard of living within the Confederation.

Helium Mining
The gas giant Tarron is the center of He_3 mining in the Kulu system. This operation consists of forty-plus cloudscoops controlled by fifteen asteroid settlements in orbit around Tarron. In addition to the Tarron operation, each of the principality systems possesses a gas mining operation. The cloudscoops supply all of the Kulu Kingdom's industrial, civil, naval, and transport energy requirements, as well as supplying fuel for visiting starships.

The price of He_3 within the Kingdom is equal to the

price which the Edenists charge throughout the Confederation, and is an arrangement of sheer necessity. If Kulu He_3 cost more than Edenist fuel, its industry would suffer accordingly. The Kulu mining operation is profitable, although its dividends are not as high as more normal commercial activities. The colossal scale of the operation makes up for this one shortfall, and the Saldana family considers it a more than worthwhile price to pay for complete independence. Starting with King Richard, they have always viewed the Edenist energy monopoly as a gross incursion of their national sovereignty. However, He_3 is not exported by the Kingdom, since the Kulu Corporation simply could not match the lower price the Edenists can charge for He_3 in star systems without a developed mining industry. Nor would there be many star systems willing to pay the political price of having their energy supplied by the Saldanas. The Kulu Kingdom is one of the very few examples of a sovereign state possessing its own He_3 mining operation and, now that star-system colonization is conducted on an almost institutionalized basis, that seems set to remain so. The two other principal exceptions are Oshanko and Far Texas. Ironically, the only other nation-state to possess its own cloudscoop is Tranquillity, which assumed control of the Kulu Corporation's Mirchusko mining operation when it became officially independent from the Kingdom. Yet none of these mining operations pose any real threat to the Edenist energy monopoly.

Currency

The Kingdom uses a decimal pound as its currency. Most transactions are done through credit disk, though the Royal Mint does issue silver and gold sovereigns. During "private" events, such as a night out at a restaurant or club, senior-echelon Saldanas can pay any bills with a platinum crown, equal to £100. Issued only to members of the family, needless to say these coins become instant collectors' pieces, and can subsequently change hands for twenty to thirty times their actual face value.

As with the Edenist dollar, He_3 has given the Kulu pound an enviable stability, and its exchange rate against the fuseodollar has remained unchanged since 2370. Thus the pound is the second strongest Adamist currency (after the Govcentral dollar), and the Kulu Crown Bank is a prevailing influence across the Confederation.

Kulu Royal Navy

Kulu maintains the third largest naval force in the Confederation, after Earth and the Edenists, with 750 warships on active service. The Saldana family is a strong supporter of the Confederation, and one-third of the Royal Navy remains on permanent assignment to the Confederation Navy, with each squadron serving six-year tours of duty.

The naval squadron deployment levels throughout the Kingdom systems, and a willingness to pursue pirates (assisted by the Fleet Intelligence agency) across Confederation territory, have made the Kingdom systems the safest in the Confederation through which to travel, after the Sol system.

Intelligence Services

Kulu's intelligence-gathering activities are divided between three agencies, all of which are funded by taxes paid to the court, and controlled by the most senior privy councillors. The King himself chairs the inter-agency management council. The three agencies are as follows.

1. Internal Security Agency (ISA)

This deals with threat assessment and threat elimination within the Kingdom itself. Contrary to public opinion and tabloid media speculation, it is the smallest and least active of the three agencies. It monitors all senior politicians and their parties for signs of disloyalty, as well as monitoring radical groups and any other organization or individual that could conceivably threaten the stability of the Kingdom or pose a physical threat to the senior Saldanas.

It has agents operating on every planet, and in every asteroid settlement within the Kingdom. Their primary task is the collection of information and, unlike the police, they do not require a warrant to search public or private data cores, or to intercept communications.

Threat elimination is conducted with as little fuss as possible. The Saldanas do not favor trials, which give their opponents needless publicity. In political cases, direct evidence of unsavory activity, or data carefully leaked to the media, is nearly always successful in halting the career of subversive individuals, neutering the threat they pose. In the case of radical groups, particularly those sanctioning and practicing violence, deportation to a Confederation penal planet (from which there will be no return) is the preferred option. In these cases, deportation orders are issued directly (in camera) by the Lord Chancellor upon request by the ISA chief, and are not subject to appeal or judicial review, the offender being simply removed from public life as quietly as possible. The secretive nature of their forbidden activity means they are unlikely to have a large collection of colleagues querying their abrupt decision to "emigrate."

Actual assassination of the state's internal enemies is a last resort, and practiced only on people who have already killed for their cause, or are known to be in the process of sabotage.

2. Fleet Intelligence

Basically this is an anti-piracy operation run by a senior admiral. Its members are Royal Navy officers who go undercover by signing on as crew on likely trader ships, i.e. those fitted with antimatter drives (see Starships, page 65). Their principal task (along with the CNIS office) is to locate pirate antimatter stations as well as the suppliers of illegal combat wasps, and those networks through which pirated cargoes are distributed.

A second function of Fleet Intelligence is to monitor the developments in naval technology by other governments.

3. External Security Agency (ESA)

The largest and by far the most active of these three groups, the ESA has agents working on every planet in the Confederation, hundreds of independent asteroid settlements, and the five independent bitek habitats, gathering strategic, political, and commercial data. Station heads in the Kulu embassies run networks of recruits, who infiltrate every aspect of their host government's civil service, including, where possible, its intelligence arm. As with the Saldanas, who take a long-term view in their policies, the ESA prefers to recruit university students and junior politicians and then allow them to work their way up the promotion ladder (often with covert assistance), rather than target established officials for purposes of subversion. The influence which this agency exerts upon foreign governments is immense. In several instances even a foreign government's head of state has been secretly working for the ESA.

A special effort is made by the ESA, whenever carrying out its investigations in the star systems immediately around the Kingdom's boundaries, to ensure that policy remains non-confrontational in terms of the Kingdom itself. Several principality leaders have been toppled by the ESA once they showed signs of "standing firm" against the Kingdom in the matter of trade (the Kingdom being a vigorous exporter) or diplomatic policy.

There is no Confederation planet exempt from ESA activity, and the exposure of any of its agency "assets" has occasionally led to diplomatic incidents, which the Saldanas inevitably ignore until the fuss dies down several decades later. Only the Edenists are immune to manipulation by the ESA, as it is impossible for the agency to turn any Edenist into one of their assets.

3. The Principality of Ombey

Ombey, a planet fifty-seven light-years from Kulu, is the most distant—and newest—planet in the Kingdom, discovered in 2467, confirmed as terracompatible and opened for immigration in 2470.

Star System Physical Data

The system is composed of eight planets, four of them solid and four gas giants, as well as two asteroid belts. The star is a G4 type.

There are four solid planets.

	Colonia	Ombey	Mauro	Celebres
Orbital distance from star (million km)	90	142	211	782
Diameter (km)	8,300	13,150	11,420	7,200
Atmosphere	—	oxygen/ nitrogen	oxygen/ carbon dioxide	nitrogen
Atmospheric pressure	—		3	5
Moons	1	1	2	5

Planet	Moons	Orbital distance from planet (km)	Diameter (km)	Atmosphere	Atmospheric pressure
Colonia	captured asteroid				
Ombey	**Jethro**	485,780	1,095		
Mauro	**Roth**	89,000	900		
	Eduis	237,000	1,800		
Celebres	captured asteroids				

There are four gas giants.

	Arorae	Nonouit	Tarawa	Abaiang
Orbital distance from star (million km)	603	1,320	2,936	4,766
Diameter (km)	53,000	138,000	47,000	42,000
Ring systems	—	1	1, huge	12
Moons	6	32	17	

The first asteroid belt orbits between 59m and 65m km out from the star. It is a narrow but dense belt, with 321 asteroids over 150km in diameter, and 18 asteroids 1,000km plus in diameter. The largest asteroid, Gamow, is 1,350km in diameter.

The second asteroid belt orbits between 325m and 560m km from the star, with a more normal density distribution. It has no asteroids over 50km in diameter.

The Planet Ombey

Colonization was funded entirely by the Kulu Treasury and the Kulu Corporation. It held protectorate status from its discovery in 2467 until the population reached 10,000,000 in 2512. It is now a fully fledged principality of Kulu, and enjoys full constitutional rights, with an elected Parliament to advise the Princess.

The planet has a rotational period of 24 hours 17 minutes. Its axial tilt is 2.6°; however, because of its proximity to the star, there is little seasonal variation. The equatorial zone remains hot throughout the year. The tropics extend to latitudes of 50° north and south of the equator, and beyond that there are small bands of temperate climate between 50° and the polar circles. Its year is 346 days long, and the traditional months have been shortened to either 29 or 30 days. Every sixth year is a leap year.

One-third of the planet's surface is land, and this is divided between six continents: Mario (the largest), Esparta, Xingu, Blackdust (a desert straddling 20 percent of the equator), Uatuma, polar (north), and Guarico. There are four oceans, containing a large number of islands and archipelagos. The moon, Jethro, produces moderate tides.

The capital of Ombey is Atherstone, on the eastern shore of Esparta, 5° south of the equator. Its population is 4,000,000. Kirsten, the Princess Royal, was enthroned in 2608, and holds her court in Burley Palace with her consort, Edward, Duke of Soarhime (an industrial city in Xingu).

The total planetary population is now 95,000,000, and it remains open to immigration from other Kulu worlds, and to other Christians from across the Confederation. Public hospitals support a large exowomb project for families, and four to seven children is the norm, although this trend is now dropping. Free land grants, of forty hectares per couple, and the large zones enjoying a tropical climate make Ombey a popular world to settle on, its agricultural potential attracting many colonists. Fruit is a principal product, and distillation produces some spirits and wines suitable for export. Technological exports are minimal. Imports are also kept to a minimum, to help the trade balance and encourage local industry. High-technology items such as nanonics are imported from other Kingdom worlds.

Economy

Agriculture forms the major part of the economy. The manufacturing industry can now supply the planet's farms with their complete requirements, and is beginning to expand out of its subsidized infrastructure core support activities. Many of Kulu's larger companies have offices and factories on the planet itself, though more are setting up local divisions on asteroids to take advantage of the start-up tax incentives. While still being some decades away from repaying its investment loans, the Ombey government no longer requires subsidies from the Kulu Treasury or the Kulu Corporation. Taxes levied by the Princess (as the King's representative) are paid to the King's court, but they are all spent locally on naval bases and government contracts, etc.

Comprehensive road links between the urban areas have been built, and the network is expanding. A global datanet has been established, and industrial and transport power supplies are available in all inhabited areas.

Asteroid Settlements

There are nine asteroids in orbit 120,000km above Ombey, all of them mining operations, besides a number of industrial stations owned by large Kulu companies. Now that the planet's economy has begun to expand, their output is rising proportionally, and a considerable number of new stations are being planned. Ombey does not yet have a starship-production facility, but support contracts involving licensed spares production awarded by the Royal Navy base should ensure that a fully indigenous design and construction capability develops within the next fifty years.

As yet, only twelve asteroid settlements have been established in Ombey's inner belt by Kulu companies. But the exceptionally rich mineral and metal reserves in these asteroids should eventually lead to a vast increase in activity. It was the potential wealth of the inner belt which was the deciding factor in King Lukas's decision to make Ombey a principality, rather than sell the settlement rights.

Helium Mining

There is one cloudscoop, orbiting Nonouit, with an asteroid settlement supporting the mining operation. Both are owned by the Kulu Corporation. This level of activity is capable of supplying all Ombey's current energy requirements, although capacity limits are approaching. A second cloudscoop is planned for construction starting in 2620, and major contracts will be issued to Ombey's asteroid settlements for its components.

4. Tranquillity

Tranquillity is an independent bitek habitat orbiting 587,000km above the gas giant Mirchusko. It was germinated in 2428 by the then Crown Prince of Kulu, Michael Saldana. There are no other human settlements in the system.

Star System Physical Data

There are three solid worlds, three gas giants, and an asteroid belt. The star is an F3, 1.2 times the diameter of Sol, and hotter.

There are three solid planets.

	Jyresol	Boherol	Philobe
Orbital distance from star (million km)	95	208	380
Diameter (km)	7,100	9,200	12,000
Atmosphere	—	—	nitrogen with hydrocarbon traces
Atmospheric pressure	—	—	7
Moons	1	2	—

There are three gas giants.

	Delila	**Mirchusko**	**Iarvid**
Orbital distance from star (million km)	850	1,700	3,200
Diameter (km)	162,000	151,000	32,000
Ring systems	1, substantial	Ruin Ring; inner ring	
Moons	27	27	11

Principal moons:

Planet	*Moon*	*Orbital distance from planet (km)*	*Diameter (km)*	*Atmosphere*	*Atmospheric pressure*
Delila	**Tylvio**		10,500	nitrogen	
	Abellia	130,000	160	—	—
	Balota	147,000	95	—	—
	Choisya	232,000	2,850	—	—
Mirchusko	**Dianthus**	390,000 (a ring shepherd)	400	—	—
	Erinus	583,000 (Ruin Ring shepherd)	800	—	—
	Falsia	1,200,000	2,890	—	—
	Galtonia	3,065,000	620	—	—

Mirchusko has a ring of debris from wrecked alien habitats, in a 580,000km orbit called the Ruin Ring (see below). There is a second, inner ring, orbiting between

370,000km and 390,000km (shepherded by Dianthus), where the blackhawk eggs grow.

The asteroid belt orbits between 420m km and 630m km from the star.

Tranquillity

History

The star system itself is unremarkable, and was first visited in 2420 by a Kulu Royal Navy scoutship, the *Ethlyn*. Routine survey probes revealed the Ruin Ring, which generated considerable interest among the xenoc researchers across the Confederation. There was no trace of the Laymil race who had lived in the habitats, nor was there any trace of them on any of the solid planets or gas giant moons. The combined Royal Navy and Nova Kong University team which was sent to investigate estimated that there were anywhere between 50,000 and 70,000 Laymil habitats orbiting Mirchusko, and that they all disintegrated at the same time: 2,400 years previously, plus or minus twenty-five years. Remaining particles range in size from dust motes up to habitat shell sections 200m in diameter, but fragments had been retrieved on a see-and-grab basis, and clearly any long-term archaeological investigation project would be required to reach full understanding of the tragedy.

Kulu filed a settlement claim on the system with the Confederation in 2422. It was at this point that Crown Prince Michael began to take a personal interest in the

Ruin Rings. The motivation behind his interest was never fully explained, but there are two probable reasons.

The first possibility is that he became obsessed with the causes of the habitats' disintegration. It is widely supposed that the Laymil underwent a mass suicide, since an accident on such a scale is virtually inconceivable for a race of their technological advancement, and fragments of records found since then have strengthened this theory, so it may well be that he wanted to know if the human race could ever find itself in a similar position.

The second reason suggested is that he deliberately used the Ruin Ring to initiate conflict with his own family. The prospect of a life of 160-plus years dedicated solely to public service, when one's every second has been planned weeks or even years in advance, is not something readily acceptable to everyone, even someone enjoying the privileges accorded to the Saldanas. Prince Michael may have seen the discovery of the Ruin Rings as his escape from another hundred years of excruciating boredom. He was sixty-seven at the time and his father, King James, was already ailing. Whatever the reason, he instigated a vast research project into the Laymil. Against all tradition, and with near-total family disapproval, he ordered the cloning of a bitek habitat from Tropicana (even he wasn't radical enough to approach the Edenists for one) and had it germinated on an asteroid orbiting 587,000km above Mirchusko. He also diverted considerable Kulu Corporation funds to con-

struct a cloudscoop so that Tranquillity and its support
stations would be completely self-sufficient.

While bitek is the logical solution to supporting a
community devoted to academic research in an isolated
star system, its use was a severe breach with accepted
Christian ethics (because of its association with affinity). Michael then compounded his crime by using neuron symbionts to establish an affinity bond with
Tranquillity. After this, he ordered a modified affinity
gene to be spliced into the DNA of his own son, Maurice, so that the boy would also be able to communicate
with Tranquillity. This last act, committed in 2432, the
year his father King James died, was the last straw as far
as the Saldana family was concerned. Michael, in so
blatantly disregarding his role as defender of Christianity in the Kingdom, was clearly unfit to rule. He was
thus never crowned, and his brother Lukas became King
instead.

Michael and the infant Maurice were excommunicated, and banished to Tranquillity (Michael's wife,
Princess Ginevra, did not accompany him to Tranquillity but went into exile on Avon, supported financially
by the Saldana family until she died in 2487), and the
habitat was granted to them as a dukedom in perpetuity.
In 2440, Michael declared independence from the Kulu
Kingdom, and no attempt was made by Lukas to reclaim
it (possibly a situation planned for by Michael, since it
would have been politically difficult for the King of
Kulu to reclaim a bitek construct, not to mention one
owned by his elder brother). So Michael became known

as the Lord of Ruin, a title Maurice assumed on his father's death in 2513.

Cut off from the virtually bottomless funding of the Kulu Corporation and the Royal Treasury, and alone in a star system with no terracompatible planet, and with only eight industrial stations, financial expediency became paramount (certainly in the early years), and the original research project into the Laymil and their suicide was considerably downgraded. However, Michael went on to establish Tranquillity as an important trading station, a blackhawk base, outsystem banking center, and tax haven (see Economy, page 133), so that foreign currency earnings were maintained, which he could then continue to spend on the research to which he had devoted his life.

The Lords of Ruin

Michael   2440–2513
Maurice   2513–2601
Ione   2601–

Ione was gestated in 2593, in a womb-analogue organ similar to those used by voidhawks. Maurice is known to have had several other children (conceived naturally), all of whom left home to become Edenists. Maurice wanted to avoid the situation where several rival candidates would be eligible to control Tranquillity. But the modified affinity gene he carried (and passed on to all his children) is also capable of the Edenist general affinity.

Economy

Michael's triumph in making Tranquillity financially viable is a feat almost equal to that of his celebrated forebear, Richard, which is a fact not overlooked by historians specializing in the Saldana family.

After the declaration of independence in 2440, Tranquillity's population numbered 17,000, consisting of Michael's personal retainers (who had remained loyal), the xenoc research staff (only 20 percent remained after the declaration, the rest going back to Kulu), the cloudscoop crew, and a skeleton crew manning the industrial stations, plus a few Royal Navy officers responsible for the strategic-defense platforms (most of whom had been blacklisted anyway). Turning such a motley collection of resources and people into a successful mini-nation was by any standards nothing short of miraculous.

With no outstanding debts on the cloudscoop, Michael offered He_3 at a price 10 percent lower than the Edenists, turning Tranquillity into an important port for starships in that sector of the Confederation. He wrote a simplified version of the original Kulu constitution, which was enforced by the habitat consciousness. Such an Adamist-Edenist culture combination proved popular, especially with the relaxed banking laws Michael included in his constitution, and so immigration began. Low taxes and a guaranteed crime-free environment, as well as the notoriety of Michael himself, helped attract the wealthy to Tranquillity. The habitat soon began to prosper as a trading and finance center. Finally he offered Tranquillity as a base for blackhawk mating flights, an action which turned the habitat into the premier blackhawk port in the Confederation, eventually supplanting Valisk. Several prominent astronautics companies have established industrial stations to support the starships calling at Tranquillity, and most of the multistellar corporations have offices inside the habitat.

The Habitat

Tranquillity follows the structure, general layout, and internal functions of Edenist habitats; however, at 65km long, and 17km wide, it is the largest so far germinated in Confederation territory. It orbits 590,000km above Mirchusko, outside the Ruin Ring, and has the usual band of starscrapers around the center, 500m long. The cavern climate is sub-tropical, and there is a circumfluous saltwater reservoir at one end, 8km wide and 300m deep, with several islands. The central cavern vegetation is a mixture of many different kinds introduced from terracompatible planets across the Confederation.

There are two voidhawk/blackhawk docking ledges on the endcap, with radii of 2.5km and 5km respectively. The non-rotational spaceport is a disc 4km in diameter, supported by an axis spindle 3km long; it is powered by fusion generators, and does not receive electricity from the habitat induction cables. The maw endcap is orientated to galactic south (corresponding with Mirchusko's magnetic field). The population in 2610 is 3,100,000.

Tranquillity was designed to support 5,000,000 people, so while there is no need yet for a second habitat above Mirchusko, one will eventually have to be germinated if its population continues to expand at the current rate. Since it will have to be funded by the Lord of Ruin, this notion gives credibility to the considerable speculation of a new Saldana dynasty arising there.

Habitat Consciousness

This is the principal difference between Tranquillity and an Edenist habitat. While able to communicate with Edenists using affinity, the consciousness is answerable only to the Lord of Ruin himself. There is no multiplicity since, on dying, the Lords of Ruin choose not to transfer their memories into the neural strata, nor will the personality accept the memories of dying Edenists (though it will store them for retrieval by voidhawks should an Edenist die while resident). It is a singleton mentality.

As with Edenist habitats, the personality provides the civil administration and financial service, and in these respects is incorruptible. However, as the inhabitants are not Edenists, a physical security construct has been included in the habitat servitor genealogy. The personality, in conjunction with the Lord of Ruin, is reasonably tolerant of wayward human behavior, but comes down hard on major transgressions. The habitat contains a great number of rich immigrés essential to the economy, and their peace of mind is paramount.

The Tranquillity Sergeants

The sergeants act as a police force for the habitat personality, enforcing the law. They are not individually sentient, but are controlled by the habitat personality, and their brains are forms of bitek processor circuitry enabling them to perform simple functions such as patrolling and observing without constant supervision. They are also responsive to the Lord of Ruin, who can use his or her affinity to direct them, but they do not receive affinity commands from Edenists.

Sergeants are humanoid bitek constructs, 2m tall with a reddish-brown exoskeleton, their joints covered by segmented rings allowing limbs full articulation. Their heads have a sculpted appearance, with the eyes concealed within a deep horizontal gash for protection. There is a mouth with a hinged jaw, but no teeth; the nose is a simple oval inlet hole between the mouth and eye gash; each ear is a hole at the center of a petal pattern on either side of the head. Their hands have five fingers and a thumb, enabling them to use any equipment designed for humans. Their feet have no toes, however. They have the ability to talk, though individual units simply relay whatever the habitat personality itself wishes to say, normally informing wrongdoers of which law they have broken, why they are being arrested, etc.

Sergeants digest a special protein paste exuded by the habitat food-synthesis organs. They have no sexual traits, and their eggs are produced inside an ovary organ within Tranquillity's servitor facility. The hatchery is contained in caverns in the southern endcap and, after they hatch out, sergeants take fifteen months to reach full size, living for approximately fifty years.

All sergeants are armed with nervejam sticks; projectile or beam weapons are only issued in times of emergency. Their size and threatening appearance are often enough in themselves to quell any disturbances in pubs and clubs.

Tranquillity Defense

When Michael took control of Tranquillity, the Royal Kulu Navy left behind seven strategic-defense platforms, capable of providing close-range cover around the habitat. The cloudscoop anchor asteroid was protected by its own beam weapons.

Since then the Lords of Ruin have extensively upgraded the SD platform network as the starship traffic requirements have expanded. Manufacturing and service contracts are awarded to astroengineering companies which have local stations, and Tranquillity is now self-sufficient in its defense requirements. A 100,000km emergence exclusion zone is in force around the habitat. Like Edenist habitats, Tranquillity is linked into the defense net via bitek processors, and runs it without human intervention (with the exception of the Lord of Ruin). Maintenance is performed by locally based companies.

The habitat personality also monitors the Ruin Ring to ensure that starships are not engaged in illegal scavenging operations. If one is found, then either a blackhawk will be contracted to intercept, or if the starship jumps outsystem before interception, a Confederation regional law violation alert will be issued, empowering national governments and navy vessels to apprehend the offending ship, with no statute of limitations.

Blackhawks are usually hired by Tranquillity should any naval-type action be required (specifically anti-piracy), and a store of combat wasps is maintained for this purpose. The simple presence of so many black-hawks in the star system should be deterrence enough to Adamist starship pirates. The blackhawk captains do show a certain loyalty to the Lord of Ruin for opening Tranquillity as a base for mating flights. And, of course, Tranquillity supplies the blackhawks with the nutrient fluid they digest.

The Ruin Ring

The ring is actually fairly small in cosmological terms. The main section is a band 3km thick and 70km broad, which orbits 580,000km above Mirchusko. Small parti-cles extend some 100km either side of the main band, tapering away from the center. The ring is shepherded by Erinus, orbiting at 583,000km, which is largely re-sponsible for its stability.

Ring particles are made up entirely from the debris of the Laymil habitats, which includes shell sections, soil, ice crystals, petrified vegetation, mummified animal and Laymil bodies, artifacts, etc. All of the larger parti-cles are extremely fragile due to vacuum evaporation. Certainly animal or Laymil bodies cannot be touched without extreme care, and finding an intact corpse is very rare. It is estimated that this gradual decay process will abrade all these particles down to sand and dust within another 3,000 years.

The Laymil

Substantial remains have been recovered, and a comprehensive picture of Laymil physiology has been built up. They were a three-gender race, with two males and one female (two sperm carriers, one egg carrier), but there was some distinction between the two males. They were trisymmetric, standing approximately 1.75m high, with three legs, three arms, and three sensor "heads."

The head resembled a terrestrial serpent's, with a breathing and speaking mouth equipped with olfactory sensors; above that was a single eye, and an ear was positioned on top. One mouth was larger than the other two, suggesting that although all three could form sounds, one of them was more fully developed, thus giving a broader vocal range. Their necks were small and thick, all three sprouting from the top of the torso. The digestive mouth was in the cleft between these necks, and was equipped with needle-sharp teeth.

Their arms possessed a single elbow, and a shoulder socket that permitted considerable range of motion. There were four fingers, triple-jointed, 10cm long. Each leg featured a single knee-joint, and the foot ended in a hoof; vestigial toe-bone remains suggest that these had evolved considerably from their pre-sentient form.

The female grew some kind of sac below her torso to contain her three embryos (one of each sex), and she would appear to have been immobile in the last stages of pregnancy. A female was capable of reproducing up to five times (see The Laymil Research Project, page 143), but it is not known if the social unit was marriage as practiced by humans. At least, housing units within the habitats were always equipped for three adults. Laymil were warm-blooded herbivores breathing an oxygen-nitrogen atmosphere, and evolved in a 0.85 standard gravity field. Their skin color was a light grey, and they wore clothes but no shoes.

It may be that the Laymil had performed some genetic engineering on themselves, as a sequence similar to the human affinity gene has been identified in their DNA. Tranquillity geneticists are studying the prospect of Laymil clone production in an attempt to bring the species back to life, since enough DNA samples have been located to provide an adequate gene pool.

The Laymil Habitat
The Laymil habitats had a similar layout to Edenist habitats in that they were cylindrical, 50–60km long, and used induction pick-up cables as a power source. Although the outer shell was made of a tough layer of silicon similar to the monobonded hulls of starships, this may have been secreted by the living inner structure. If so, Laymil genetics were considerably more advanced than human bitek. There were no starscrapers, and no food-secretion organs. The Laymil ate the vegetation grown in the central park. Both endcaps had long spires extending 15km along the axis, with an outer layer of photoradiant cells emitting a spectrum identical to the local system's star, with only the infrared band reduced. Taking this into account, the climate inside the habitats must have been sub-tropical.

All animal species shared a common structure, i.e.

they all came from the same planet. So did all the plants. No insects have yet been discovered.

As far as can be ascertained, the habitats destroyed themselves. The cells of the living, inner structure underwent some kind of convulsive spasm, cracking the silicon shell. The conclusion must be made that this convulsion was deliberate, since every habitat was destroyed in a period of approximately fifteen minutes. If it was the result of some weapon used against them, it had to be extraordinarily powerful. No evidence has yet been uncovered to counter the theory of suicide.

Laymil Spacecraft

The remains of several spacecraft have been found, all of them interplanetary fusion craft with artificial organs providing life-support functions. There is no evidence of the Laymil ever building FTL starships. This raises the fundamental question of where the Laymil originated from, as no planet in their local system ever evolved any life form. The current conclusion is that they came to the system in a multigeneration arkship in a similar fashion to the Tyrathca, although this itself has not been discovered.

Their spacecraft fusion drives used He_3 as a fuel, so it is inevitable that some kind of mining operation was conducted in Mirchusko's atmosphere, yet no remnants have been found. If it was a cloudscoop venture, then the orbit of its anchor asteroid would have started to decay as soon as it stopped operating. And it is extremely doubtful that any aerostate would survive intact for 2,600 years in a gas giant's storms. No detailed search for one has been conducted so far.

Scavengers

Scavenging the ring is an occupation followed by upwards of 3,000 inhabitants of Tranquillity. There is no standard craft used; vehicles vary from MSVs with strap-on auxiliary engines to adapted ion-field flyers (the ion field gives some protection from dust abrasion).

Pilots drop down from Tranquillity into the ring, or slightly above it, and try and spot any interesting item there. As 95 percent of the mass is habitat-shell material, this is very much a hit-or-miss activity. The normal procedure is to find a section of the inner shell and explore it for artifacts. Records (the Laymil used a solid-state crystal for storing data) are the most valuable find, followed by manufactured items and animal or Laymil bodies (only two Laymil bodies have ever been found intact since 2420).

The Lord of Ruin does not allow starships to scavenge the Ruin Ring (there are some transgressions, but all minor ones). All finds must be returned to Tranquillity, where the scavenger will usually hand them over to an auction house. Laymil artifacts fetch enormous prices, right across the Confederation. The legendary "big find" is the basic motivation for most scavenging. However, Tranquillity itself has the right of last bid in all the auction houses; after the price for an item has been agreed Tranquillity can then match that price plus 5 percent to secure the item. In this way, the habitat's research specialists can acquire the most interesting and unusual items without having to employ their own teams to scour the rings.

The Laymil Research Project

There are some 3,000 specialists on xenoc culture, covering all disciplines, working for the Lord of Ruin on interpreting items scavenged from the ring, and building up a picture of Laymil life. As well as humans, six Kiint are involved with the project in order to provide much needed alternative viewpoints. All findings are eventually released to universities across the Confederation, but the Lord of Ruin reserves the right to restrict military technology.

They have had considerable success in re-creating the physical parameters of both biological and technological aspects; which means they know the mechanics of the Laymil, but their culture remains somewhat veiled. The scarcity of records is mainly responsible, since the solid-state storage crystals have been badly damaged by 2,600 years of exposure to vacuum, and few coherent bytes remain.

The Laymil electronic technology was equal to that of the Confederation circa 2300. Decrypting their programming language was completed in 2495, and accessing the storage crystals became relatively easy after that. Their written symbols are geometrical: circles, triangles, and squares, either singly or in combined pairs, some with cross-strokes and dots. Their alphabet has thirty-two separate characters. Grammar and syntax follow a logical formula, and a vocabulary of 25,000 words has been established.

Naturally, examples of writing have so far been of a technical nature, relating to the equipment that each storage crystal was part of. No paper, or paper analogue, has yet been located.

The Laymil possessed some arts, mainly painting and sculpture, although interpretation of these is difficult. No recordings of music have been found.

Only three examples of Laymil speech have been found, which together last for just seventeen minutes. They had deep voices, employing many guttural sounds. Most of the words employed have been identified, although the sounds blend together since they did not appear to separate these words in the human fashion. The subjects of the three recordings are what appear to be:

1) an exchange between a spaceship pilot and some kind of flight controller;

2) a discussion involving five Laymil, on how a habitat interior could be improved;

3) the recital of a family tree, where every member is assigned an economic value.

Mirchusko Helium Mining

The original cloudscoop was retired in 2550, after a replacement was constructed. The Edenists offered Maurice Saldana a partnership, but he refused and raised the finance from an interstellar banking consortium instead (including the Jovian Bank), and the loan should be paid off by 2625. The scoop itself was built at Jupiter, and the anchor asteroid refinery came from the O'Neill Halo, with subcontracts spread across the Confederation. No Kulu Kingdom companies bid for any of the contracts.

One cloudscoop is quite sufficient to supply the habitat industrial stations and visiting starships. The present cloudscoop has a design life of 125 years.

5. Avon

Avon is a terracompatible planet ninety-three light-years from Earth. An ethnic Canadian world, it was discovered in 2147, and opened for emigration in 2151.

Star System Physical Data

The Avon star system has five solid planets, and two gas giants, and there is a single asteroid belt. The star is a G2 type.

There are five solid planets.

	Haslemere	Sarlowe	Rhus	Avon	Drnask
Orbital distance from star (million km)	49	72	101	143	258
Diameter (km)	3,200	8,000	9,000	12,500	15,000
Atmosphere	—	—	reducing	standard	nitrogen-hydrocarbon
Atmospheric pressure	—	—		1	4
Moons	—	1	5	1	3

The asteroid belt orbits between 305m and 470m km from the star.

There are two gas giants.

	Ocymum	Celosia
Orbital distance from star (million km)	598	875
Diameter (km)	140,000	115,000
Ring systems	1, small	—
Moons	8	17

Avon

Physical Data

Avon has one moon, Nepeta, 3,000km in diameter, with an orbital altitude of 437,000km. It has a thin carbon dioxide atmosphere, and the surface is lightly cratered.

Avon's gravity is 0.97 standard. There are eight continents, covering a third of the surface. Rotation takes 23 hours 32 minutes. The year is 350 days long, with a leap year every three years. The capital is Regina, with a population of 8,000,000. The planetary population is 834,000,000.

History

Avon has progressed along almost standard lines. Its first century saw the dumping of 73,000,000 people there by Earth's Govcentral. The economy was essentially agricultural throughout this time, and it wasn't until 2230 that real industrial development began.

The constitution is standard for a democratic republic. It provides for a Parliament on each continent, and an overall planetary Parliament with a president. Avon does not have a state religion. There is an independent judiciary.

In 2271 Avon hosted a summit for the planetary heads of state, called in response to the increasing use of antimatter as a weapon, and has served as home to the Confederation Assembly ever since. There are over 1,500,000 accredited diplomats and their staff, providing a substantial boost to the local economy. As well as the Assembly compound, the Confederation Navy has its main headquarters in Trafalgar, orbiting 110,000km above the planet. This asteroid was moved into position by the Avon government, and handed over in its entirety to the Confederation. Avon corporate orbital industry stations provide the systems to maintain the asteroid, and Avon companies performed the civil engineering work needed to produce the caverns.

Economy

Avon's economy has benefited enormously from the Confederation presence. Planetary service industries support the Assembly compound and the embassies. The asteroid settlement industry stations are heavily (though not exclusively) involved with Confederation fleet contracts. As a consequence, the starship manufacturing capability among the local asteroid settlements is almost as advanced as Earth's and the Kulu Kingdom's.

There are fifteen asteroid settlements in orbit around the planet (including Trafalgar), and eighty-four independent settlements in the asteroid belt. The asteroid settlement population is 15,000,000.

The safety provided by basing the 1st Fleet in this system means that piracy has become essentially non-existent, which in conjunction with the large influx of starships on government business has helped establish Avon as a substantial port in its own right.

He₃ Mining

There is a large Edenist presence in the Avon system, orbiting Ocymum. There are twelve cloudscoops mining the gas giants, providing fuel for the copious starship traffic as well as the rest of the system's industrial facilities.

The cloudscoops are tended by twenty-five bitek habitats, which possess a considerable number of attendant industrial stations. Many joint commercial enterprises have been formed with the Adamist asteroid settlements, and Avon companies. The Edenist population is 45,000,000.

Trafalgar

Trafalgar is a stony-iron asteroid, approximately the shape of a peanut, 11km long, and 4.5km at its widest. There are three cylindrical chambers hollowed into it, each 3.5km long and 1.5km in radius. All of these support numerous caverns. It has two large spherical counter-rotating spaceports, and three docking ridge ledges at each end for voidhawks and blackhawks. The asteroid has no attendant industrial stations like ordinary asteroid settlements.

Legally, the asteroid is Confederation territory and the First Admiral is its governor, responsible for all civil and military aspects of its operation. There is no internal industry or economy, all supplies coming from the Avon system, although there are protein vats which can support the population in an emergency.

Trafalgar is home to the Navy Academy, which trains all career officers. It also houses the principal Marine training barracks.

Its population is 80 percent transient. There are many civilian employees providing basic engineering and administrative services, and a small entertainments and leisure activities trade flourishes, mainly restaurants and clubs for off-duty personnel. These establishments are usually Avon company franchises. For long-term leave, naval personnel normally visit the planet itself.

The civilian contract worker population is 125,000, and the naval personnel 190,000 (including 1st Fleet crews).

6. Lalonde

Lalonde is a terracompatible planet 319 light-years from Earth. Colonization is open to both humans and Tyrathca.

Star System Physical Data

There are five solid planets and five gas giants. The star is a G7 type. There is one asteroid belt.

The solid planets:

	Calcott	Gatley	Lalonde	Plewis	Coum
Orbital distance from star (million km)	52	92	132	215	6,500
Diameter (km)	4,340	18,000	11,800	7,500	6,370
Atmosphere	—				
Atmospheric pressure	—	15.7	0.93	0.003	0.7
Moons	—	6	3	3	2

The asteroid belt orbits between 372m and 485m km from the star.

There are five gas giants.

	Murora	Bullus	Achillea	Tol	Puschk
Orbital distance from star (million km)	989	1,490	2,629	4,310	5,780
Diameter (km)	169,000	147,000	107,000	89,000	75,000
Ring systems	—	—	—	—	—
Moons	37	27	29	18	9

Lalonde

Physical Data

The planet has a rotation period of 26 hours 19 minutes, and a year of 295 days. Gravity is 0.91 standard. There is a 7° axial tilt which, combined with its proximity to the star, gives Lalonde a hot climate. The equatorial zone is uninhabitable by humans, and sub-tropical climate extends to the polar regions. There are no ice caps. The one (northern) polar continent, Wyman, has a slightly cooler climate, but is subject to severe storms when the cool air and arid hot air fronts clash. Humidity is high right across the planet.

There are three moons. The innermost, Rennison, is airless, 1,300km in diameter, with an orbital altitude of 275,000km, giving it a period of fifteen days. It has been heavily cratered, and possesses a grey-brown regolith. The second innermost, Beriana, is 900km in diameter, with an orbital altitude of 397,000km, giving it a period of twenty-nine days. It has a few large craters, and is a dull yellow in color. The outermost moon, Diranol, is 4,800km in diameter, with an orbital altitude of 520,000km, giving it a period of thirty-five days. It is very similar to Mars, with an iron oxide regolith, and a thin carbon dioxide atmosphere.

The tides produced by these three moons, especially when in conjunction, are very powerful, and low-lying coastal areas are regularly flooded, leading to the extensive evolution of saltwater-resistant plants.

One-fifth of Lalonde's surface is land, and there are six continents: Sarell (equatorial), Wyman (polar),

Amarisk (northern, the largest), Clopton, Knape, and Mosedale.

Only Amarisk is inhabited. It covers an area of 6m km^2, with fold mountains—the Puttack range, in the east, leading down to savannahs in the west. The largest river, the Juliffe, is 1,900km long, with a tributary network rivaling Earth's Amazon. The capital city is Durringham (population 175,000), situated at the mouth of the Juliffe, on its northern bank (the river being 12km wide there). The planetary population is 12,000,000 including 850,000 Tyrathca.

History

Lalonde was discovered in 2576, and opened for colonization in 2582. After the scoutship which discovered it put the settlement rights up for sale, they were bought by a venture company which went on to form the Lalonde Development Company. The LDC attracted enough funding to mount a biological survey, which was completed in 2578, clearing the biosphere for human colonization. At this point the LDC was floated on the O'Neill Halo stock exchange, looking for full start-up fund investment. Shares were optioned by the following companies:

12 percent Lithcoine astronautics, registered in the O'Neill Halo.

10 percent Miconia industrial, registered in the O'Neill Halo.

8 percent Forvoit mining, registered on Avon.

15 percent Sandering Civil Engineering, registered on New California.

7 percent Nares industries, registered on Argonne.

5 percent the Jovian Bank.

2 percent the Royal Kulu Bank.

10 percent the Tyrathca government central economic council.

31 percent held by various trusts, banks, and individuals, with no such holding exceeding 1 percent.

Lalonde is officially a EuroChristian ethnic world, and Christian missions are granted land by the Development Corporation governor. Although open to all people who fall within its ethnic stream, the LDC recommends that immigrants should have geneering that enables them to withstand the strong UV light of the sun. The Tyrathca immigrants are all farmers, cultivating the rygar crop (see Vegetation, page 157).

With so many stage-one planets currently open for immigration, the Lalonde Development Corporation had a lot of trouble attracting funding for start-up. Without Tyrathca support it is unlikely the project would have got off the ground for several decades more. (There are over twenty-five terracompatible planets that have passed their biological clearance review by the Confederation Xenobiological Hazard Assessment Board, and are waiting colony start-up funds from the owners of their settlement rights.)

It is rare for a planet to be opened on a budget quite as small as that which the Lalonde Development Corporation has available. However, it has achieved most of the criteria required for successful colonization, though the standard of living for its population is generally lower than equivalent planets.

The Lalonde Development Corporation is responsible for law enforcement and civil administration until 2670, or when the population reaches 75,000,000 whichever comes first. Town councils (for towns with a population over 7,500) with the authority to pass local bylaws will be permitted from 2625 onwards; county councils after 2635; state councils after 2650. Until then, towns and counties are run by company managers who are only obliged to "consult" with any local bodies. Newly established villages (with small populations) are given a settlement supervisor by the Development Corporation, who is responsible for upholding the law in his or her district as well as advising on agriculture and building construction. The LDC also employs marshals (inevitably combat-boosted) to quell any major disturbance and track down groups of outlaws in the countryside outside Durringham.

Tyrathca settlements are run along standard Tyrathca clan lines. There are no joint settlements.

Economy

Lalonde is still in its first development stage, and the society is primitive. The majority of human immigrants to date have been people wishing to farm. The Development Corporation gives each immigrant (over nineteen years old) seventy-five hectares, and children of settlers are also entitled to seventy-five hectares when they too reach the age of nineteen. Because of the competition between colony worlds (in 2610 there are thirty-nine of them accepting immigrants), the Development Corporation decided to accept category 3 convicts (non-lethal) as involuntary transportees from Confederation planets (mostly from Earth).

The Tyrathca came to Lalonde exclusively to farm the rygar crop, which grows only in mountainous regions. There was a large initial batch of breeders, with a small retinue of vassal castes, who arrived in 2585. They settled the Puttack Mountains, where they form an isolated community of their own. Starships chartered by the Tyrathca Central Economic Council to maintain contact have VTOL spaceplaces capable of bypassing Durringham spaceport and landing directly at the Tyrathca settlements.

Human colonists are now progressing further up the Juliffe River for their land grants, and are establishing villages close to the Tyrathca, though there has been minimal contact so far. The constitution allows for distinct habitation areas for both races, ceding most mountain ranges to the Tyrathca and ensuring natural segregation so that inter-species incidents are kept to a minimum.

The Tyrathca do export some of their crop to their homeworld, Hesperi-LN, but this trade makes little impact on Lalonde's planetary economy as a whole. There are no metalled roads or rail networks. Transport is centered around the Juliffe and its tributaries, with a considerable quantity of river traffic (another factor in favor of reduced-cost colony start-up). To encourage boat building, the Development Corporation provides loans for thermal-exchange furnaces and electric motors to power ships constructed out of native timber. Durringham has a flourishing shipyard industry.

So far, 90 percent of all human settlements have been made on the banks of the Juliffe and its tributaries.

There is little manufacturing industry in terms of machinery and electrical goods on the planet, and none at all outside Durringham. Those manufactured goods which are produced are basic implements for households and farming, and solar-cell roofing panels. One company, Parry Engineering, has started to make powerbikes capable of using the mud tracks between villages. With several service companies maintaining the engines and equipment used by the larger ships, it is expected that future industrial growth will be led by that sector in conjunction with requirements for mechanized farm machinery.

The planet has no communication net, not even in Durringham. There is a communications satellite permitting a minimum of communication between the governor's office and LDC representatives in the countryside.

One asteroid, Kenyon, has been maneuvered into orbit, 112,000km above the planet, but mining machinery has not yet been shipped in there. A caretaker station owned by the Development Corporation is attached. This whole asteroid project can only be regarded as highly premature.

There are no independent asteroid settlements.

The Edenist Habitat

In 2602 the Edenists germinated Aethra in orbit above Murora, and it will be fully grown in 2630. There is no cloudscoop, and there is almost no He_3 usage at all in the system. Durringham has a few generators, principally for the spaceplanes which bring colonists down from their starships. All their He$_3$ is imported.

A small inhabited station with thirty personnel is maintained in orbit around Murora to monitor and assist Aethra's growth. Crew duty tours are five (Earth) months, and a voidhawk visits every six weeks from the Jospool star system, the nearest fully developed system, eight light-years away.

Vegetation
As a stage-one colony, Lalonde is heavily reliant on its aboriginal plant species for many aspects of everyday life. Some are integral to the local economy, while others are highly detrimental.

Kerriaiweed
A tenacious reed which grows in the low-lying coastal areas, and can withstand being submerged in salt water. It has a mat root system to hold the sandy soil together.

Mayope
A very slow-growing riverbank tree with big scarlet flowers and black bark. It requires a wet soil. The wood is extremely hard, and difficult to ignite, making it ideal for constructing both buildings and ships. Logging operations are extensive, as is the sawmill industry which has built up around heavy demand. There is considerable worry that this resource will be badly depleted in another thirty years, and the governor is encouraging sustainable forestry initiatives. Because of mayope's

slow growth rate, it is doubtful that this will be a practical solution.

Cherry oak
A tall tree with white bark, its leaves are small, and the fruit resembles an acorn in shape, but bright red. It is edible, with a nutty taste.

Gigantea
A tree with an outer coating like thick mauve-brown coconut hair instead of a true bark. Its branches all slope downwards, and the leaves are pale green. It requires deep moist loam to grow in, and is prevalent close to rivers and lakes. Heights of up to 220m have been recorded, with trunks in excess of 40m in diameter on the largest specimens. The LDC governor has given these all preservation status, and felling them for timber is strictly prohibited.

Vines
There are two hundred different species of vines growing in the forests. The most important are:

Tinnus, blue flower, fast-growing ground cover.

Acillus, yellow flower, green fruit, tree climber.

Isonar, big (1m) scarlet and blue flower, fast-growing ground creeper.

Danzar, small dark purple tubular flower, white fruit, poisonous, tree.

Canus, a small evergreen plant with a four-month cycle: when cut and dried, it can be smoked as a mild hallucinogen.

Foltwine, freshwater aquatic, like a thick brown ribbon, very slippery. It grows so thickly in some places in the Juliffe that it impedes boat traffic. Boats with cutting cables stretched between them patrol regularly to keep navigation channels open in shallow areas, and are funded by the Development Corporation. Any swimmers who get caught in foltwine escape with great difficulty.

Snowlily, freshwater aquatic. Its baseplants grow along the side of the river, and produce a large (2m) white saucer-like leaf with a kernel at the center. When it is mature, the leaf will detach and float downstream until it snags, then it roots. Lasting for about ten days, this happens twice every (local) year, in February and August. The entire Juliffe tributary network is planted with snowlilies, and the last 500km of river becomes a solid mass of white leaves during each flowering season. All travel along this section is suspended during that season: the sheer proliferation of snowlilies makes the use of any kind of boat impossible. Consequently, river captains have petitioned the governor's office for a virus that will kill off the baseplant, but this request has been repeatedly refused, such ecocide being strictly forbidden by the Confederation. Thus there is no practical method of ridding the River Juliffe of this hazard.

Elwisie, edible fruit (for humans) cultivated extensively. A short (3m high) tree with yellow leaves, and a 10cm diameter spheroid fruit with a thick dark purple skin. The fruit has a peach-like pulp, and can be eaten either cooked or raw.

Rygar, edible berry (for the Tyrathca), regarded as a

delicacy. It grows in bush form, producing clusters of green berries which gradually solidify into a solid nut-like sphere. These are then picked, their shells peeled, and the center ground up. The Tyrathca use the powder for making beverage drinks or for mixing with sugar to create a fudge.

Animals

The animals follow a standard evolutionary pattern. There are fish, amphibians, and mammals, and all are two-gender. The mammals are quadrupeds, and most possess tails, but their hands or paws have six digits. Fur has not evolved, so scales or smooth hide is the norm, to allow cooling in the planet's hot climate.

Kroclion

A large (4m long, 1.7m high) carnivorous animal with dark grey-green scales, it is a highly territorial jungle dweller (occupying an area of roughly 5km^2). It bears some resemblance to the Earth crocodile, but its legs are longer and the hindquarters taper down to a long (3m) whip-like tail. It can reach only a steady trot, but once it is running very little can stop it, normal jungle under-growth posing no problem. It eats vennal and sayce (see below), and will also attack humans and Tyrathca, though a large amount of xenoc flesh will poison it. Al-though the kroclion is a jungle dweller, it does not like the kind of excessive humidity found by the rivers, thus making the inhabited lands relatively clear of this prob-lem so far. However, when the colonists start to expand out from the river margins, kroclions will start to pose a problem.

Vennal

A herbivore tree dweller (1m tall), with exceptional dexterity. There is no distinction between fore- and hindpaws. The tail is well developed and assists it in climbing. There is a faint resemblance to a lizard, and its skin is a blue-green hide.

Sayce

Dog analogue: a carnivore similar to a cat with black scales. The paws have six sharp claws to help it climb trees. It is impossible to domesticate a wild sayce, but those raised in captivity become obedient to human vocal orders. Very rudimentary vocal cords allow limited response, and sayces can manage about fifteen to twenty words. This ability of response does not qualify it as sentient under Confederation classification rules. Any words need to be taught by a competent handler, and cover set situations such as *"help," "danger," "come," "go,"* etc. A sayce can also learn the names of its human family.

There is a considerable sayce-racing fraternity, and meetings are held in most villages. An underground sayce-fighting organization also exists, which the Development Corporation does very little to discourage.

7. Norfolk

Norfolk is a terracompatible planet 247 light-years from
Earth. An English-pastoral-ethnic world, it was discovered in 2207, and opened for colonization in 2213. It is
unusual in that the star system is a binary.

Star System Physical Data

There are two stars, six solid planets, no gas giants, and
a considerable number of asteroids. The primary star is
Duke, a K2 type (cooler than Sol). The secondary star is
Duchess, an M5 type (red dwarf). Duchess orbits
around Duke at a distance of 372m km, giving it an orbital period of 1,425 days, or approximately four
(Earth) years.

Four of the solid planets are in orbit around Duke.

	Derby	Lincoln	Norfolk	Kent
Orbital distance from star (million km)	49	130	173	212
Diameter (km)	3,800	5,100	11,200	9,300
Atmosphere			standard	
Atmospheric pressure			1.08	
Moons	—	1	2	3

The remaining two solid planets are in orbit around
Duchess. They also form a binary of their own, the separation distance being 570,000km.

	Westmorland	Brenock
Median distance from star (million miles/km)	17/27	17/27
Diameter (miles/km)	2,600/4,183	1,990/3,202
Moons	—	—

The main asteroid belt orbits between 45m and 72m miles (72m and 114m km) from Duke. There is a smaller belt orbiting between 28m and 32m miles (45m and 51m km) from Duchess. There are secondary belts between all the planets orbiting Duke, and a large number of rocks which exchange stars every few centuries. In addition, there is a large quantity of comets and small, pebble-sized particles loose in the system.

Norfolk

Physical Data

Gravity is 0.87 standard, axial inclination 1.7°. Orbital rotation around Duke takes 452 days, however its year is 659 days (see climate, below). Planetary rotation is 23 hours 43 minutes.

Atmosphere is 77 percent nitrogen, 22 percent oxygen, 1 percent carbon dioxide, resulting in air which feels heavy. New arrivals find it moderately difficult to breathe, acclimatization taking several days.

Just over 40 percent of the surface is land. There are no continents in the normal sense, and very little tectonic activity. Most of the land mass is made up of large islands, 40,000 to 60,000 square miles (100,000 to 150,000km²) each; the rest comprises small archipelago chains in the seas between the islands. There are few mountain ranges. Because of this geographical structure, the open-water areas are not large enough to qualify as oceans, so there are only "seas."

Regarding climate, the seasons are not decided by the planet's orbital period but by the time it takes to reach *superior* conjunction between Duke and Duchess (every 659 days), and they are experienced uniformly over the planet. The distance it orbits from Duke would normally give Norfolk a permanently cold climate; however, the infrared radiance from Duchess, as it approaches superior conjunction, produces a warm summer equivalent to normal terrestrial temperate regions. During the height of summer the hours of darkness gradually reduce to zero (midsummer).

Winters are uniformly cold, with *inferior* conjunction removing Duchess from the sky altogether. The temperature will sink to –77°F (–25°C) at midwinter, and thick snowfall is planet-wide.

The capital is Norwich, on the island of Ramsey, with a population of 970,000. The total planetary population is 324,000,000.

Norfolk has two moons.

Argyll is heavily cratered, and has a dull grey regolith.

Fife's surface is made up entirely of ice 10–25m thick, which is subjected to considerable tidal stress, and is severely cracked. There are no craters. A thin lower level of water exists around volcanic vents. Some surface melting occurs when Norfolk reaches superior conjunction between Duke and Duchess. Very primitive bacteria live in the water.

Moon	Diameter miles (km)	Orbital distance from planet in miles (km)	Atmosphere	Atmospheric pressure
Argyll	1,120 (1,802)	161,500 (259,854)		
Fife	2,000 (3,218)	298,000 (479,482)	thin carbon dioxide	0.03

Constitution

The planet has a pastoral/Christian constitution which limits the manufacture, import, and use of advanced technology. An official list of acceptable technological items is maintained by the government, and can only be added to by a 70 percent vote in favor in Parliament.

Government is an elected planetary Parliament, with a Prime Minister. Each island has its own council, and local authorities are modeled on the old English structure circa twentieth century, with county, town, and parish councils. There is an independent judiciary.

A hereditary constitutional guardian from the Mountbatten family is responsible for seeing that both Parliament and the judiciary don't overstep their constitutional limits. Because of its ties with old England, there is a titled and landed aristocracy, headed by the Mountbatten prince. The House of Mountbatten is proud of its links with that most modern of monarchies, the Saldanas. In 2380, a (natural-born) daughter of King

James married the Mountbatten heir, and the family has subsequently promoted the idea of a "special relationship" with the Kulu Kingdom.

There is no House of Lords, though inevitably the aristocracy is wealthy enough to have considerable unofficial influence over local matters. Many of its members sit on local councils.

History

The *Duke of Rutland* scoutship entered the Norfolk star system in 2207. Biological certification was achieved in 2210, and the Norfolk Land Company opened the planet for colonization in 2213. Because of its unique situation, a constitution was written to attract settlers who were dissatisfied with the technoeconomic life prevalent elsewhere throughout the Confederation. The planet was an ideal site for such a group: without a gas giant to mine for He_3, no asteroid industry would develop, and it is the only place where the famous Norfolk weeping rose will grow, providing the planet with an income capable of paying for the few advanced technology items it needs to import. The planet was opened to volunteers only, and there have never been any involuntary transportees on Norfolk. The government claims this is the primary reason why the crime rate has remained low (well below the Confederation average) throughout its history. The constitution also permits anyone to emigrate, a clause written in order to prevent people dissatisfied with the pastoral lifestyle from having to stay there against their will and therefore possibly causing trouble. It should be noted, however, that the average Norfolk laborer would take a very long time to earn enough money to buy passage out on a starship. The government doesn't subsidize emigration, though that concept has been raised several times in Parliament.

Succeeding generations have adopted their original ancestors' work ethic, thus making Norfolk as prosperous as any pastoral planet can be. Immigration continues, though at a much reduced rate, typically 10,000 per (Norfolk) year. Because of the low level of medical technology, most immigrants have tended to be those with considerable geneering in their ancestry. Illness is consequently rare, leaving hospitals free to concentrate primarily on accidents. Although medical nanonic packages are proscribed, most medicines are permitted, and nearly all injuries are survivable.

Technology

The list of prohibited technologies is a long one. Basic-level electronics is permitted, but nanonics are banned completely. Didactic education is not employed, and the university syllabus is strictly controlled, while there is very little research permitted. Higher education subjects tend to be practical rather than theoretical.

The limitations of medical technology are the biggest cause of argument among the population, and the question of drugs and treatments to be permitted is the one area of the prohibited list which is constantly under review. Parliament consequently votes for expansion of the medical list at least once every session.

Planetary communication is by landlines only, and the net is very rudimentary. It is used principally for voice-only telephone services. Though some data can be carried, the bit rate is extremely low. There are no sensorium broadcasts. 3D AV (audio-visual) broadcasts are the standard entertainment medium.

Satellites exist to link visiting starships into traffic control, and enable them to establish contact with the ground.

Aircraft are permitted, though they are limited to emergency services. There is no civil aviation transport industry. Spaceplanes and ion-field flyers may only use designated spaceports.

The only spaceplane registered to Norfolk is owned by the state communication company, and it is employed to maintain the communication satellites. Its crew are foreign workers.

There is no commercial docking station in orbit, and no facilities to perform maintenance on visiting starships. If a starship is in need of repair, its captain would have to arrange for the parts, crew, and any necessary service machinery to be shipped in. More than one starship line has been bankrupted by mechanical misfortunes at Norfolk.

There are no indigenous spaceplane operators. Starships wishing to transport Norfolk Tears (see Economy, page 170) must ship it up in their own ground-to-orbit vehicles.

The principal form of ground transportation is by train, which requires an extensive network of tracks. Every town and most of the villages have their own station. The tracks are simple twin rails, and the trains themselves are powered by electron-matrix crystals.

The trains are designed to run throughout the year, and are fitted with snowplows for Norfolk's winter.

There is a small road system on most of the islands, with metalled surfaces connecting major towns and cities. Over the rest of the countryside, farm tracks of crushed stone provide transport routes between farms and towns. Few of the metalled roads remain viable during midwinter, when snowdrifts can reach 3m in depth. Some of the richer farmers use powered vehicles, but there are very few private cars, so the horse and carriage prevails in rural areas. Though powerbikes are popular with the younger urban inhabitants, ordinary bicycles remain the norm.

A good range of agricultural machinery is produced by local engineering firms. All of this machinery uses an electron matrix powering electric engines. Because of their complex molecular structure, all electron-matrix cells have to be imported.

Power

Norfolk is unique in having absolutely no fusion generators at all. Power for industrial consumers, urban areas and agriculture is produced from geothermal exchange cables, an imported solid-state fiber which uses the temperature difference between deep hot rocks and the cool surface environment to generate current directly. These cables are a high-technology product, but they are permitted because importing He_3 would cost too much and would require a sophisticated support infrastructure. Hydroelectric power is impractical on any reasonable scale, due to Norfolk's geographical make-up, since the islands simply don't have the kind of extensive mountain ranges necessary, nor is it uncommon for entire rivers to freeze solid during winter. However, the geothermal stations are non-polluting, and the cables last for centuries, so they were seen as the perfect solution for Norfolk.

There is a distribution grid of high-temperature superconductors to carry power over the islands, and in some cases between them. Domestic power requirements, especially for the isolated farms, come from solar-cell roofing panels.

Economy

The principal economy is geared around production and export of Norfolk Tears. This alcoholic drink comes from the weeping rose which, because of Norfolk's unique double-sun summer that ripens the flowers, has proved almost impossible to grow anywhere else. All attempts at this have produced a vastly inferior drink, and even chemical synthesis is difficult, leaving Norfolk as the only real source. Norfolk Tears has been described as the perfect alcoholic beverage, a pale yellow liquid with a mild dry taste that few people can resist, and it produces virtually no hangover. Norfolk Tears is exported right across the Confederation, and the price increases in proportion to the distance from Norfolk of its eventual destination. Adamists and Edenists alike provide a huge market which could easily absorb a hundred times the current production level. (The Saldanas send a ship each season so that their royal table is never without a good supply.)

Roughly 65 percent of farms cultivate the weeping rose as their primary crop, though almost every rural cottage possesses a small grove of its own. Production is organized on a regional basis, with local producers sharing a single bottling plant. Each grove carries its own label, though there are also blended varieties. There is a government-run growers' association which sets a minimum price (taking foreign earnings requirements into account), and Tears is always bottled on the planet itself, adding to its cost of shipment.

Most major Confederation banks have branches on Norfolk to facilitate its foreign currency exchange. The planet's entire foreign earnings occur annually in a single twenty-day period just after midsummer.

The government prohibits a futures market (which would become dominated by large offplanet commercial companies), and the Tears crop is only available to starships actually visiting the planet at the time of its sale, preventing the development of a monopoly situation by large commercial fleets. Norfolk wants the supply of Tears to be spread as widely and thinly as possible, half of the product's appeal being in the mystique of its scarcity.

Naturally, as there is only one crop every 659 days, the number of starships arriving then is extensive—upwards of 25,000.

Because demand for Tears always outstrips the supply, starship captains try very hard to establish lasting bonds with the agents of regional production groups in order to secure their cargo. In this way, a strong underground futures market has developed, with cash bribes and prohibited technology being offered as sweeteners.

Defense

Norfolk's other significant aspect is that it is the only developed planet in the Confederation not to possess a strategic-defense network. The reason for this is that the only thing of value on the planet, or indeed in its whole system, is Norfolk Tears, which simply cannot be snatched away by spacefaring pirates.

However, starships jumping outsystem are vulnerable to interception when they are carrying valuable cargoes of Norfolk Tears, so a Confederation Navy squadron is assigned to the system for an anti-piracy operation during each midsummer. Norfolk is a fully integrated member of the Confederation, and meets all the expenses incurred with this protective deployment. After each operation, the crews enjoy shore leave, attending formal parties thrown for them by all the major Norfolk cities during which each guest is traditionally given a specially labeled bottle of Norfolk Tears by the local growers' association, which makes participation in this anti-piracy exercise popular with all the navy crews.

This annual arrangement is complemented by the location of a Confederation Navy office on the planet, and there are usually one or two navy ships on routine patrol deployment inside the system to deter any attempt at blackmailing Norfolk through planetary bombardment by pirates.

Plants

Weeping Rose
The most famous plant in the entire Confederation is a rambling bush which produces yellow-gold blooms 25cm in diameter, with a thick ruff of petals around an onion-shaped carpel pod. At midsummer the flower always droops over, so that when it is fully open it faces towards the ground. As the seeds ripen, the pod exudes a fluid which is collected and fermented in wooden casks for a year, then bottled. Only after the new-year crop is safely in will the previous year's vintage be released.

The pods exude (weep) all their fluid within just thirty-six hours, leaving a dry carpel which then splits open to throw out the seeds. The Weeping Rose is usually cultivated on a wire, and pruned to a height of 3m. A mature (third-year) plant will produce up to twenty-five flowers. The fluid is collected in waxed paper funnels positioned round each plant, and an experienced grower will always be able to tell exactly when the flowers are about to weep.

Grass-analogue
This is remarkably Earth-like, except that its leaves are tubular and produce minute white flowers throughout the summer. The flowers can only be triggered by a double-star spectrum.

Trees

There are a number of evergreen species, resembling the terrestrial pine. Their leaves are also usually dark and narrow, although much thicker. There are no cones, as they reproduce by spores. All the islands contain extensive forest areas.

Earth crops

Wheat, barley, oats, potato, maize, and most other Earth-originated vegetables have been geneered for use on Norfolk. The grains are capable of producing two harvests during the superior conjunction season, though a degree of care must be taken in storing them during the long winter. There are no aboriginal grain plants. Other terrestrial plants such as trees and canes have proved difficult to modify for the double-star spectrum and the particularly long year.

Animals

Evolution has produced surprisingly few land animals. There are some fish, though again the variety is lower than usual. Mammals are two-gender quadruped marsupials with an ordinary biochemistry. All have thick shaggy fur, and considerable subcutaneous fat to survive the long winters. Hibernation is common.

Hax

This wolf-analogue is a small (1.2m long), feral beast, a warren dweller. Its hind legs are powerful, enabling it to bound along in long leaps. Its typical litter is three pups, and it hunts in packs. The hax is not intelligent enough to be domesticated, and they often attack humans, especially during winter when food is scarce. Local hax hunts with hounds are well established, and provide farmers with sport during the winter months. Most inhabited areas have been cleared of them, but where woodland and moors provide cover they can still be a problem in even the longest-settled areas.

Snakerat
This rodent, with small legs and a long sinuous body, is similar to a ferret and has a mildly poisonous bite.

8. Nyvan

Nyvan is a terracompatible planet fifty-eight light-years from Earth. It was settled in 2134, early in the Great Dispersal, and as such was one of the last planets to receive immigrants under Govcentral's equal ethnic representation policy. Initial development was funded entirely by Govcentral and until the Land Liberation conflict in 2257 it was referred to (by its inhabitants) as the Last Imperial Colony.

Star System Physical Data

The Nyvan star system has two solid planets and a single gas giant. There is one small asteroid belt (as yet uninhabited). The star is a G3 type.

There are two solid planets.

	Nyvan	Josquin
Orbital distance from star (million km)	107	576
Diameter (km)	11,200	9,000
Atmosphere	standard	—
Moons	1	3

The gas giant is Linicus.

	Linicus
Orbital distance from star (million km)	865
Diameter (km)	128,000
Ring systems	3
Moons	17

Nyvan

Physical Data

The moon, Almore, is 3,900km in diameter, and orbits 320,000km out. The tides it produces are large, and have turned many coastlines into marshland areas.

Nyvan's year is 372 days long. The planet has 0.91 standard gravity. Planetary rotation is 24 hours 39 minutes. Axial inclination is 2.2°.

Forty-one percent of the surface is land. There are seven main continents: Dayall, Kiernan, Fumiko, Mestal, Unarian, Hopeborne, and Nangkok. The climate is of a standard range, and both Mestal and Unarian extend into the polar circles. There is considerable volcanic activity on all continents. The population is 320,000,000.

History

As with all worlds colonized in the period before ethnic streaming was introduced (pre-New California 2163), Nyvan has a checkered past. There was a great deal of conflict between various ethnic groups crammed together in towns and cities, which on several occasions erupted from mere civil unrest into armed battles. The last major (global) conflict was the 2257 Land Liberation War, where resentment against Govcentral colonial governance policy (essentially limiting the land grants and forcing ethnic integration) and hostility between ethnic groupings compelled to live together combined into outright rebellion. Attacks on Govcentral buildings and staff resulted in a complete withdrawal of Govcentral involvement from the planet. As Nyvan had very little industrial or technological capability at that time, and certainly did not have a starship-manufacturing capacity, all contact with Earth and the rest of the colony worlds ceased for seventeen years. (The system as a whole was not isolated; the Edenists naturally maintained contact with their habitats orbiting Linicus.)

During this time there was a massive redistribution of population, resulting in the formation of twenty-three separate nations. Each of these new nations was based around a single and separate cultural or religious ethic.

Although the Govcentral administration had tried to distribute ethnic groups evenly, concentrations invariably arose, and these formed the nuclei of the emergent nations.

Migration was a constant feature of Nyvan life for over a decade; it is estimated that over 70 percent of the population ultimately shifted in search of sanctuary. Initially this was from choice, then, as living conditions and racial violence worsened, people sought out their own kind in self-defense. In the latter few years as the nations established themselves, and very stringent (in some cases virtually fundamentalist) constitutions were written, racial expulsions, purges, and deportation became commonplace.

The hardships of this time were appalling. No modern transport infrastructure existed. Some continental railway lines were still in use, although they were inevitably the target for partisan troops. The planes had all been conscripted and adapted to military functions. Some four-wheel-drive farm vehicles were in use, but again these proved useful for the military. People traveling either used horses or walked; even ocean-going ships were wooden-hulled, and over half of them used sails rather than technological propulsion. Given that the distances they had to travel to find a nation of their own ethnic grouping could be up to half a world away, it is not surprising that an estimated 4,000,000 died on the journey. All those who moved and survived had meanwhile lost their homes and farms, and businesses which had taken their families decades to build.

The enmity engendered by this migration and nation-forming period was so virulent that to this day it has not abated. Several nations still do not even consider establishing diplomatic relations. After the principal phase of migrations finished in 2270, boundary skirmishes continued to be fought for another 115 years, costing another 750,000 lives.

Today, four major nations dominate the planet: Isfahan, an Islamic republic; Tonala, a democratic republic; Nazareth, a Christian republic; and New Georgia, a federal union.

The circumstances this world now finds itself in are not favorable—a situation which has come about entirely because of the multitude of uncooperative nations it hosts, which is almost unique in today's Confederation where most worlds are single-state cultures. It is less developed than 90 percent of Confederation worlds, and its intrinsic nature means it is likely to remain so for the foreseeable future.

Most telling of all, there is no record of immigration for the last two centuries, while emigration, typically 50,000 a year, is constant. As only an estimated 10 percent of the population has the financial or political ability to buy themselves a ticket off-world, and it is inevitably the most talented who leave, in doing so, by taking away the very people (middle-class professionals) most needed to accelerate the planet's development, this further reduces the possibility of Nyvan becoming anything other than a backwater.

Isfahan

With a population of 50,000,000, this is an Islamic culture run entirely by the mullahs through a conclave. Theirs is not even a token democratic government, but a highly fundamentalist regime maintaining technology at early twentieth-century levels—with one exception, weapons, which are imported. Education is severely limited, and no didactic technology is allowed. The general population is not allowed to come into contact with foreigners, nor are foreign nationals allowed entry apart from company sales agents. Details on conditions outside the cities are sparse, but it is probable that rural inhabitants know little of the Confederation at large.

All trade is conducted by state-appointed representatives; and what little foreign currency is earned is invariably spent on weapons and medical nanonic packages for senior mullahs. Isfahan has taken over the entire Nangkok continent, absorbing three other nations in the process. They regard Tonala as their principal enemy, and view that nation's slow but sure technoindustrial growth as threatening. Of course their own culture prevents them from matching this kind of advancement; which means that Tonala, with its starships and strategic-defense platforms, will always have military superiority, although invasion and conquest of Isfahan is not a serious option.

Isfahan refuses to acknowledge the authority of the (moderate) Confederation Islamic Congress, which in turn regards this nation's extremist fundamentalism with considerable embarrassment.

Nazareth

With a population of 47,000,000, this is a pastoral-technology culture. There is in fact a Parliament, but all the political parties are orthodox Christian in persuasion, so few new laws are ever passed. Everyday life is very settled there. The nation occupies the central swath of the Hopeborne continent, a position which gives it an overall temperate climate. The land is very fertile, supporting a vast number of small farms.

Again technology is kept to a minimum, with the exception of medical systems (good Christians could hardly refuse aid to an injured person). Most of the money Nazareth's agricultural exports bring in is spent on importing advanced medical supplies from the Confederation (the system's Edenist habitats are Nazareth's major trading partners). Although they permit free access to visitors, their own population is discouraged from foreign travel, and few would have the financial resources to do so anyway.

A reasonable road and rail infrastructure exists, and electricity comes from a mix of geothermal, tidal, and wind sources. Industrial capacity is modest, supplying most of the nation's needs. Little money exists for imports. The press is reasonably honest, although very parochial. There is no modern communication net, only a telephone system.

Tonala

With its population of 32,000,000, Tonala occupies two-thirds of the Dayall continent. Its capital is Harrisburg. Although technically a democracy, it is firmly run by the Free Union Party, which has been in power for the last 180 years. Power swings between the wings of the party, and internal maneuvering decides the leadership. This is Nyvan's most industrially advanced nation, although its socioeconomic index is roughly equivalent to a stage-three colony planet (one developing an astronautics capability, normally reached 150 years after colonization).

There is a vast disparity of wealth, with the top 5 percent of income earners leading extremely luxurious lives. Corruption is rife, with industrial baronies effectively in charge of the country. It is they who raise money for, and principally control, Free Union. These companies are desperate to earn foreign currency, and ensure that little restriction is placed on military exports, for which there is always a market. Although Tonala companies hardly build the most sophisticated armaments in the Confederation, there is a constant demand from semi-legal groups or various independence movements who need weapons to further their cause.

Military development contracts, and national conscription, have ensured that Tonala possesses the most powerful armed forces on the planet, including a small strategic-defense capability.

Two asteroids, Kotok and Pringle, were moved into low orbit by the Opia company. They are being mined for metal and minerals to supplement planetary reserves, and an astronautics industry is slowly developing along standard lines. Initial contracts are all heavily supported by the state, and collaborative ventures are being sought with major multistellar companies. A commercial starship-maintenance capability already exists. Some military ship refitting can be carried out by the industrial stations.

New Georgia

Having a population of only 20,000,000, this is the smallest of the "big four" nations, and is established to the south of Nazareth. It was set up by emigrants from the old USA, and has re-created a sizeable portion of its constitution. It comprises sixteen separate states, five of which are nothing more than industrial cities. It has a reasonably advanced industrial base which includes an orbiting asteroid settlement, Jesup. There is a standing army, and a small SD network.

Planetary Government

There is no single (UN-equivalent) agency. Instead there are political or defense alliances based around the four major nations. Only Tonala, New Georgia, and Nazareth have any interest in the Confederation. Tonala has a non-voting membership (they pay a token 1m fuseodollars per year) equivalent to a stage-one colony world, and both New Georgia and Nazareth have observer status.

Planetary Defense

Tonala's navy has three frigates, bought second-hand on very favorable terms from Kulu. They are over forty years old, and require a great deal of maintenance. Their asteroid industrial stations have the capability to manufacture combat wasps.

Tonala has a nominal defense cooperation arrangement with the Edenists. But the lack of any serious firepower and sensor networks makes any starship visiting the system vulnerable to pirate activity.

There are few strategic-defense platforms in orbit. The networks which exist were established not so much to defend the planet from an external threat as to monitor the near-space activities of other nations and protect their own land from orbital bombardment. Most of the starships owned by "national" commercial fleets are combat capable.

Edenist Habitats

There are seven habitats orbiting Linicus, with a combined population of 8,000,000. Again this unusually low number reflects the dismal performance of the planet as a whole. Other (more successful) planets colonized around the same time have up to thirty habitats.

There is only one cloudscoop, which supplies enough He_3 for the system and all visiting starships. The Edenists themselves consume 25 percent of its output. Although Tonala is at last beginning to develop its technology base, and starship trade is gradually increasing, it is estimated that a second cloudscoop will not be required for at least another eighty years.

9. The Dorados

The Dorados is a vast, dense ring system orbiting a red dwarf star, Tunja, which includes 387 large asteroids (>40km diameter) with a near-pure metal content. Tunja is 235 light-years from Earth. There is no terracompatible planet in the system. Planetologists believe the Dorados and their associated belt are the result of a collision between a Mercury-sized planet and a very large interstellar meteor. Over 200 of the Dorados are roughly spherical, indicating that they were core magma material when the collision took place, and subsequently solidified in their current shape.

Star System Physical Data

The Dorados system has one gas giant planet and one asteroid belt. The star is a M4 type, a red dwarf.

The asteroid belt orbits at a median distance of 40m km from the star.

The gas giant is Duida.

	Duida
Orbital distance from star (million km)	40
Diameter (km)	48,000
Ring system	—
Moons	8

Dorados

Physical Data

In order of settlement:

	Mapire	Ayacucho	Yavi	Maturin	de Apure	Barinas	El Toouyo
Diameter (km)	78	65	87	76	94	70	82
No. of bioshpere caverns	4		3	2	2	2	1

The capital is Mapire, with a population of 450,000. The total Dorados population is 1,300,000. All the settled asteroids orbit in a zone 1m km in diameter, near the inner edge of the belt.

History

The star system was first explored in 2579, by whom is not known exactly. Both Garissan and Omutan scout survey ships claimed they were first to discover these extraordinarily metal-rich asteroids.

The dispute over discovery, and consequently who had settlement rights, escalated into a war which ultimately ended in the Garissa genocide, when Omuta launched a series of antimatter planetbusters at Garissa.

Subsequently, the Confederation Assembly awarded possession and all rights connected with the Dorados to the Garissan survivors, of which there were nearly 2,000,000. Some of the survivors moved to the system; these were mostly the civil servants and other government officials, along with industrialists and financiers. They formed the administrative core of the Dorados Development Authority, and opened the system to Confederation companies wishing to exploit the tremendous wealth inherent in the asteroids.

The DDA is the civil government for the entire system (excluding Edenists), collecting taxes from the industrial manufacturing consortiums, and mineral extraction royalties from the mining companies. After governmental costs have been met, all the remaining revenue is annually distributed on an equal-share basis to the Garissa survivors across the Confederation. In 2610 this dividend amounted to 38,000 fuseodollars per person.

Given that their development only began thirty years ago, the progress on the Dorados so far has been exemplary. The ore is so metal-rich that it barely needs refining, allowing industrial stations to utilize it directly, eliminating the costs usually associated with building and operating refinery stations.

It is the DDA's stated policy to develop the Dorados system into the major supplier of astroengineering alloy in this sector of the Confederation. It is a policy acknowledged by financial analysts as easily achievable.

A great many multistellar companies have offices and stations in the Dorados, and expansion is proceeding apace. In all respects this is a unique system, as no other freshly discovered world or star system is ever likely to advance its industrial output so quickly. And now that its viability has been successfully proved, it is attracting a great many further companies and investors, and expansion is estimated to rise at a near exponential rate for the next century or so.

Given that the asteroid settlements are basically company towns, and there is no terracompatible planet, it is unlikely that civil development will follow the standard pattern. The DDA has no mandate to hand over government functions to an elected Parliament at any time in the future, nor is any such action planned for. However, give that the Dorados are a Confederation system, workers are granted basic civil rights. With new generations of children continually being born in the Dorados, the question of nationality is bound to rise at some time, and this issue is likely to prove a thorny one. The Garissa survivors are unlikely to relinquish their authority (and the income derived from it), and indeed they have a valid case for continuation of this situation, given their history. But certainly second- or third-generation asteroid dwellers descended from non-Garissans will in time be able to put forward an equally valid claim for an autonomous government. The argument will not be helped by the fact that these asteroid inhabitants derive from a variety of cultural and ethnic backgrounds.

Ideally the DDA should have taken this into account at the start, and at the very least limited the companies exploiting the Dorados to those from African-ethnic star systems. In view of the inescapable conflict that will arise in one or two generations' time, it would be fair to say that the plight of the Garissa survivors is not entirely over.

Economy

Naturally this is centered on producing and exporting astroengineering alloys, but basic material production is increasingly being complemented with component manufacturing, as companies invest in more sophisticated industrial stations. It is DDA policy that within ten years the Dorados will have the capacity to produce entire mining and refining stations in-system. After that they hope to build swiftly towards indigenous ZTT starship production. Most of the major multistellar companies have expressed a high degree of interest in the Dorados, and those who do not already have functioning industrial facilities there have at least got a local office. One of the largest investors in the system is the Kulu Corporation.

Transport also accounts for a large part of the economy. Inter-asteroid freight is a healthy business, with many local companies involved. Five major interstellar-line companies have port facilities in the Dorados, with their fleets supporting the bulk alloy export market. Other majors have included it on their schedules, providing regular flights out to most Confederation systems. Local spaceship companies are now starting to expand into the interstellar field, with considerable success.

Defense

With the entire output of the industrial stations marked for export, and the asteroid inhabitants providing a large market for imported food and luxury items, starship movements in and out of the system are considerable. This makes them prime targets for piracy.

Consequently, the largest single expenditure of the DDA is on defense. All the asteroids have extensive SD weapons platform networks, and the sensor network in both the local asteroid cluster and overall system coverage is first rate. A small squadron of combat-capable starships is kept on permanent patrol. Again because of the nationality issue, most of their crews are hired from outside. A large number of them are ex-Kulu Navy personnel.

Edenist Habitats

The Edenist were enthusiastic supporters of the industrial development of the Dorado asteroids. So far, two Edenist habitats have been germinated in orbit around Duida. The first, Ramtheni, is twenty-eight years old and is now mature enough to support a 50,000-strong population, a number which is reaching the top limit for such a young habitat. The second habitat is Sehad, which was germinated in 2599; initial habitability maturation is expected there in 2622.

The Edenists have so far constructed one cloudscoop, which became operational in 2585. As reflects this system's unique status, it is extremely unusual for the Edenists to begin construction of a cloudscoop before the local habitat is mature (normally no market for He_3 in any quantity exists in a system for its first century). In order to get the cloudscoop built and operational, they had to live in artificial stations, which goes against the main thrust of their culture. However, the eventual rewards of large-scale He_3 orders, to power the fusion generators in both industrial and mining stations of the Dorados, far outweighed any inconveniences meanwhile.

With the first habitat now matured, and the cloud-scoop functional, the Edenists have been swift to participate in the Dorados' industrial potential. There are over fifteen large industrial stations outside Ramtheni, and the Edenist groups have many joint-venture enterprises at the asteroids themselves.

Total Edenist population is 55,000, and a third habitat is planned for germination in 2615.

10. New California

New California is a terracompatible planet 130 light-years from Earth. It is an ethnic US Pacific-coast planet discovered in 2156, and opened for colonization in 2163. The initial development company funding was raised by the Californian State of Govcentral through a rights issue and loan guarantees.

Star System Physical Data

The New California star system has four solid planets, and three gas giants. There are three major asteroid belts. The star is a G5 type, known as Visalia.

There are four solid planets.

	Richmond	New California	Salinas	Santa Rosa
Orbital distance from star (million km)	95	146.3	237	288
Diameter (km)	6,800	12,550	5,750	6,150
Atmosphere		standard		
Atmospheric pressure		1		
Moons	2	4	2	—

There are three gas giants.

	Yosemite	Sacramento	Tehachapi
Orbital distance from star (million km)	781	1,500	2,900
Diameter (km)	157,000	115,000	53,000
Ring system			
Moons	36	23	17

The first asteroid belt, Lyll, orbits between New California and Salinas. The second asteroid belt, Piute, orbits between Santa Rosa and Yosemite. The third asteroid belt, Dana, orbits between Sacramento and Tehachapi. Both Lyll and Dana have several industrial settlements.

New California has fifty-three asteroids in orbit 150,000km above it, all moved into place from Lyll by nuclear explosions, and all now settled.

New California

Physical Data
There are four moons. Samoa and Orick are a binary pair.

Planet	Moon	Orbital distance from planet (km)	Diameter (km)	Atmosphere	Atmospheric pressure
New California	**Yuba**	190,000	1,200		
	Samoa	220,000	800		
	Orick	220,000	700		
	Requa	340,000	2,100		

New California's year is 359 days long. The planet has a 0.97 standard gravity, planetary rotation is 24 hours 7 minutes, and axial inclination is 2.3°.

Its atmosphere is 76 percent nitrogen, 21 percent oxygen, 0.02 percent carbon dioxide. Pressure is standard.

Thirty-eight percent of its surface is land. There are six main continents, Kalmath, Medford, Fortuna, Shastad (arctic), Teham, and Alturas. A group of large islands, the Santa Crutz archipelago off the shore of Kalmath, is in a climate zone similar to the old California, and is heavily populated. The climate embraces a normal range, which provides a southern polar ice cap.

The capital is San Angeles, on Kalmuth's coast, with a population of 5,700,000. The total planetary population is 890,000,000.

History

New California was settled during the Great Dispersal, and was the first planet to introduce an ethnic streaming policy, which caused some considerable controversy in the Govcentral senate at the time. However, as the early multicultural colonies were undergoing significant levels of civil unrest, and in two cases outright revolution, this screening process was eventually allowed to remain uncontested. After this, many individual Govcentral states followed suit in sponsoring their own ethnic-streaming colonies.

Originally only residents of the state of California were accepted for immigration, though this requirement has now been relaxed so that emigrants from any ethnic-compatible planet in the Confederation may apply. Immigration is now typically 35,000 people a year.

The planet is a democratic republic with a President, Senate, and Congress. Its constitution is modeled on the original American constitution, but with alterations: typically, the environmental protection clause which ensures against high-population clustering outside San Angeles (the planet pioneered asteroid metal mining and Falling Jumbo foamed lifting bodies (FJs), purely to avoid strip mining), and the permitting of "weak" narcotics. But the right to carry arms was specifically excluded. The population is mainly Christian, though, due to California's excessive numbers of spiritualist cults and evangelical missions, a number of fringe religions flourish. There is a strong constitutional proscription against Islam.

New California is one of the most successful planets

colonized during the Great Dispersal period. It has a high standard of living and a strong economy. This is due mainly to the industry which was transferred from the old California, which was always a high-technology/capitalist area. The crime rate is reasonably low, and public utility services and a socialized medical system are supported by all three major political parties.

Asteroid Settlements

There is a large population living in the fifty-three high-orbit industrial or mining asteroids above New California, all of which come under the planetary government's administration. The system's starship industry is centered here, and is supported by an above-average number of military contracts, both for the planetary navy and the Confederation Navy. Military exports to friendly systems receive good loan terms from the planetary government. A large number of commercial starships are built, along with industrial stations. The amount of metal delivered to the planet in the form of foamed-metal lifting bodies is prodigious (see History, page 199). Several of the asteroids are mined out already, so five more are currently being shifted into orbit.

Both the Lyll and Dana belts are populated. Lyll has 119 settled asteroids; Dana has 78. All of these are independent from the planetary government, though all are members of the system assembly. These independent settlements tend to concentrate on components, sub-units and maintenance rather than complete starships. Because of the high numbers of settlements and

stations, commercial competition is fierce. This has led
to some dubious exporting of items which could be used
for military purposes, and the Confederation Assembly
(acting on complaints from the navy) has censured this
export policy on more than one occasion. However,
with the system assembly dominated by representatives
from Lyll and Dana, the policy is unlikely to be changed
in the near future.

The independent asteroid settlement population is
around 30,000,000.

Technology

New California is among the top ten Adamist developed
systems, and is virtually self-sufficient in this respect. A
recent blow to local astroengineering companies was
the introduction of ion-field flyer technology from
Kulu. New California previously exported a large number of conventional spaceplanes, but production of ion-
field craft under license from the Kulu Corporation has
now been negotiated by most of the major companies.

Trade

Its industrial capacity means the system is a major trading center, with a large number of both starship and
inter-orbit ship movements every day. The number of
asteroid settlements has led to the development of a big
commercial fleet to supply their population with luxu-
ries.

The system's overall balance of payments has remained in the black for over a century.

Edenist Habitats

The Edenists have germinated thirty bitek habitats in orbit around Yosemite, to tend fifteen cloudscoops. There are a large number of industrial stations in operation at each habitat, and many joint venture enterprises have been formed with the asteroid settlements and New California companies.

The Edenist population is 50,000,000.

11. Srinagar

Star System Physical Data

The Srinagar star system has three solid planets and five gas giants. There is one asteroid belt. The star is a G2 type.

There are three solid planets.

	Obbia	Srinagar	Bomhus
Orbital distance from star (million km)	63	152	210
Diameter (km)	7,800	14,000	8,500
Atmosphere		standard	
Moons	—	3	5

Srinagar's year is 429 days long. The planet's gravity is 1.1g. In its orbit, planetary rotation is 25 hours 8 minutes, with inclination is 2°. Its atmosphere is 97 percent nitrogen, 24 percent oxygen. Pressure is 1.3 standard.

There are five gas giants.

	Kohistan	Shaidan	Kapalu	Opuntia	Parwan
Orbital distance from star (million km)	724	1,349	1,850	3,875	4,372
Diameter (km)	128,000	105,000	85,000	96,000	56,000
Ring system	3	1	—	—	—
Moons	27	25	39	22	18

The asteroid belt orbits between Bomhus and Kohistan, and it has eighty-seven settlements. Srinagar has twelve industrialized asteroids in orbit, all moved into place by nuclear explosives. Both of Kohistan's Trojan clusters have asteroid settlements.

Srinagar

Physical Data
There are three moons.

Moon	Orbital distance from planet (km)	Diameter (km)	Atmosphere	Atmospheric pressure
Juba	85,000	900		
Muri	220,000	1,450		
Batna	460,000 (retrograde)	150		

Srinagar's year is 429 days long. The planet's gravity is 1.18 standard, planetary rotation is 23 hours 8 minutes, axial inclination is 2°. Its atmosphere is 73 percent nitrogen, 24 percent oxygen. Pressure is 1.3 standard.

Forty-two percent of the surface is land. There are four main continents: Santal, Hazaribagh, Ranchi, and Sundargarth. A small island, Chamba, is arctic. The seas are populated with a number of large islands, too. The climate is generally drier than on most worlds, because of the smaller seas. The capital city is Chaibassa, on the west coast of Hazaribagh.

The principal orbiting asteroid is Dindori, which is Srinagar's main naval base and the command center for the planetary SD network.

The total planetary population is 800,000,000.

History

Srinagar is a terracompatible, Hindu-ethnic world settled during the Great Dispersal, starting from 2178. It was funded by five Indian states, which still own considerable stock in various planetary enterprises. The planet is a democratic republic, although both main political parties are heavily religious. It is quite extensively industrialized, and has a slightly below-average standard of living. Political and financial scandals are commonplace, and politically motivated violence there is above average.

There is a national Senate, continental Parliaments, and strong regional Assemblies. Although technically capitalist oriented, a great many companies are state sponsored, or partially owned by the state, through local-government development councils. These companies tend to be essential to the local economic infrastructure, such as food-processing plants in agrarian regions, vehicle factories in cities, etc. The price of this social-economic policy is such that the companies tend to lack the efficiency levels of the pure-capitalist worlds such as New California. In compensation, Srinagar has a much lower unemployment level, and a job with a company is generally "for life."

Healthcare is socialized, although the most sophisticated treatments are only available to paying customers in private clinics. Geneering is not available in government hospitals.

Technology
The twelve orbiting asteroids have a reasonable level of technological sophistication, and indigenous companies produce their own ZTT starships as well as other astronautics products. The civil astroengineering companies which capture and mine asteroids are all technologically self-sufficient; and capture-mission contracts are all tendered by indigenous companies. However, the electronics, nanonics, and cybernetics industries are not particularly strong, and the most advanced systems are nearly always built under license, notably from Edenist companies. It would also be true to say that all really advanced systems, such as those required by the navy, are produced by the Edenists or in conjunction with them.

The general level of technology in the Adamist sections of the star system is not as high as might be expected, nor is the economic output as high as in compatible Confederation worlds (i.e. those settled during the same period and with similar population levels). The principal reason for this is the star system's social/religious structure (see Religion, page 201). Srinagar is simply not party to the straightforward capitalist expansion and progress ethic which dominates many Confederation cultures, so direct comparisons with them are unfair and somewhat pointless.

Exports and indigenous sales of spaceplanes have suffered considerably in recent years due to the Kulu ion-field flyer technology. Srinagar has yet to be granted a production license by Kulu, since the Kingdom is using its technology for political advantage and, as a Hindu-ethnic culture, Srinagar is not regarded as a primary ally by the Royal Saldanas. Overall balance of payments has alternated from black to red almost year by year, though it has now remained in the red for the last seven years.

Religion

The Hindu faith remains strong among all the system's Adamists. In part this is due to the large percentage of the planetary population which lives a rural/agrarian existence (50 percent plus), with the Brahmans retaining a huge influence in tight-knit communities. The agricultural areas remain very traditionalist/conservative, and local voting patterns reflect this. Any liberal-ticket politicians are concentrated in the urban areas, and effectively marginalized. Basically, this is a society which changes very little, and those changes which do occur are slow to arrive. This situation is responsible for producing a large minority of political radicals urging change, their methods often including public protests and acts of violence or sabotage.

As always when the star system's parent planet follows a somewhat orthodox doctrine, the asteroid settlements, inevitably technology orientated, do not adhere to this faith with the same level of devotion.

Edenist Habitats

The total Edenist population is 20,000,000. There are eighteen bitek habitats in orbit around Kohistan, supporting an He_3 mining operation and numerous industrial stations. Again this relatively small number of habitats and population reflects the Srinagar system's slower-than-average economic growth rate.

Ranchi

Roughly the size of Earth's South America, the northern tip straddles the equator, but the bulk of the continent is situated in the southern hemisphere. It is divided into six large semi-arid plains separated by long mountain ranges, and there are some active volcanoes in the extreme east. One range of mountains (the highest) runs along the entire length of the north and west coasts, effectively halting cloud movement into the interior. This mountain range produces a broad strip of coastline which has a moist semi-tropical climate all year round. It is the most heavily populated area of the continent, very pleasant to live in, with many resort towns and five cities, and it is extensively farmed.

The plains lying on the other side of the mountains are very different to that along the coast. A rainy season comes to them for six weeks in every year, sweeping in from the east. The rainfall is considerable, and flooding is a frequent problem. The plains have substantial underground water reserves, which have only been lightly tapped by the local inhabitants. Several dams have been built in the mountain ranges to provide manageable water resources.

These plains consist mainly of scrub bush, with few mineral resources. Their ecology is simple and basic, with a lower than average variety of plants and animal life, but the flora and fauna which have adapted to the plains are very sturdy.

The principal reason for settlement there is the bhasri crop. This is an aboriginal plant which grows to nearly 2m tall, and produces six to eight long pods which, when ripe, can be ground down into a protein-rich flour. Bhasri is an annual plant; triggered by the onset of the rains, it grows swiftly, and is ready to harvest just five weeks after the end of the rainy season.

Of the six inland plains, only four have so far been opened for settlement; at their current rate of population growth it will take another three to four centuries before anything like full capacity is reached. Settlement follows a standard pattern, with a market or mill town serving a surrounding county of ranch farms. The town itself will be based around a bhasri-processing plant, which dries and grinds the pods. Growing and harvesting the plant is a cooperative venture between the local farming association and the state government, enjoying a small start-up subsidy provided by the national government. The finished product is then sent out to the coastal port towns by freight rail. Railway tracks remain the main transport links across the plains, since very little of a road network has been built. The state itself both builds and operates the railways.

The counties tend to be territories roughly square in shape, 150km from side to side, with the town in their geographical center. The farms radiate outwards from the town, linked only by dirt tracks, and they are separated from each other by large strips of public grazing land. All of the farms grow and harvest the bhasri crop in carefully cultivated fields, but they also keep herds of geneered cattle and goats which graze the tapweb grass that grows on the open areas of the plain. Herd numbers, and where and how often they are entitled to graze the public lands, are arranged on a voluntary basis between the farmers themselves, any disputes being arbitrated by the local farmers' association.

The eldest son will inherit the family farm, his younger brothers being obliged to start up their own farms. The government is still parceling out grants of free land, of 10km^2 each, to anyone willing to sign an agreement to keep farming his plot for a minimum of fifteen years.

Farming the bhasri plant is a relatively simple process. The fields are first prepared by mechanoid tractors before planting, and the subsequent crop is cut by mechanoid harvesters. Afterwards the remaining stalks are left to dry out, then a mechanoid tractor chops them into tiny chips, sprays them with a geneered microbe—which will break them down in the soil, adding to its nutrient base—and then they're plowed back in. Human labor tends to be mostly concerned with trouble-spotting and repairs of the machinery.

Vegetation

Manzung

There are many varieties of this bush, but all of them are a reddish brown, and grow up to 1m high, with a spherical cluster of twigs sprouting fleshy petal-type leaves, almost like a fungus. There is a deep taproot (as with most plains plants) and a thick central stem, which protects it from animals and birds by means of its exceptionally sharp thorns.

Vidor

This bush grows in the foothills, along the side of streams. It produces a human-edible fruit which resembles a prune.

Tapweb

A grass growing right across the plains, except on the driest sections or in areas with underground stone shelves that prevent subsurface water from rising. Tapweb, as its name suggests, has an extensive root network which stores a considerable amount of water, with each taproot growing 4–5m down into the soil to find moisture, and with lateral roots branching out from the crown and throwing up blades of grass, and sinking yet more taps. Its blade is relatively thick, and slightly ovoid, with a tough outer surface preventing evaporation, and will grow up to 8cm high. Seed-carrying stalks are produced during the rainy season, growing about 1m high.

Animals

Kestor
A rodent creature, longer and slimmer than a terrestrial rat, possessing black scales and a bullet-shaped head. These animals live in warrens which they dig in the soil, housing anything up to fifty of them at a time. They can prove extremely dangerous if enough of them attack at once.

Rahal
This vulture-analogue nests in rock cliffs and turrets.

Nald
A small rodent: a field mouse-analogue.

Harvor
This is a large predator and carnivore which feeds mainly off the quannier. Bigger than a dog, it is very territorial, with a red ochre-colored hide that blends in exceptionally well with the background in the plains.

Quannier
A herd animal, slightly larger than a terrestrial goat, with a dull grey hide; it is very swift. They tend to stick to the foothills in the dry season, but come out onto the plains during the rains in order to feed off the bhasri plants. This makes them a considerable nuisance to the farmers, who shoot them on sight; although the government officially disapproves of such ecocide, there is tacit acceptance of the massive extermination of them

carried out in and around settled areas. Their meat is inedible to humans, however. With their numbers declining, their predators, the harvor, are also in decline, though not quite as swiftly since they can feed off other, terrestrial, animals introduced on to the plains.

Geneered dogs

Brought from Earth by shepherds, these dogs were part of an illegal genetic program to enhance intelligence levels so that they could accept a wider range of verbal orders. They were initially developed in the early part of the twenty-first century, when affinity-bonded servitor animals were becoming commonplace. The UN and most national governments moved swiftly to end neural modification of this type, a proscription which remains in place throughout the Confederation, endorsed by Adamists and Edenists alike. Even Tropicana doesn't produce IQ-boosted animals.

Believed to be extinct elsewhere, some of these dogs rebelled against—and abandoned—their owners and formed wild packs. The farmers of the plains now shoot these dogs on sight as a public menace, and there are even local rumors of "devil dogs" snatching human children.

Valisk

The independent habitat Valisk orbits Opuntia. Despite its deterioration since Rubra's death, it remains an important economic asset to the system as a whole (see Valisk, below).

12. Valisk

Valisk is an independent (non-Edenist) habitat orbiting 470,000km above the gas giant Opuntia, in the Srinagar star system.

History

Valisk was germinated in 2306 by Rubra, an Edenist Serpent born in Machaon, a habitat orbiting Kohistan. It is 30km long and 12km in diameter. As with Edenist habitats, there is a starscraper band around its center. The climate is different from the usual sub-tropical environment favored by Edenists: scrub desert predominates one half, blending into a savannah plain before reaching the standard circumfluous saltwater reservoir at the end.

Rubra was nothing like as antagonistic and hostile as Laton proved to be almost three centuries later. He simply wanted somewhere which provided a benign environment without the stifling constraints of Edenism (a common Serpent rationale). Rubra became a Serpent at forty-four, selling his (considerable) share in his family engineering concern, and set up his own as a trader in one of the asteroid settlements in Kohistan's trailing Trojan point, owning and leasing a fleet of six interplanetary cargo ships. As this was a time of commercial growth in the Trojan point he made a considerable fortune.

After twelve years his company, Magellanic Itg, had expanded into manufacturing and mining, owning industrial stations in twenty-three industrial asteroids. Its trading arm moved into interstellar travel, with fifteen starships as well as fifty interplanetary ships. At this point he germinated Valisk, gambling his entire company by mortgaging most of it to raise the collateral he needed for cloning a habitat seed. He turned to Tropicana's biotechnology companies to produce this seed, which taxed even their considerable resources. However, they eventually succeeded, though there was a rumor at the time that somehow or other Rubra had actually acquired the DNA code for a habitat before he left Machaon (it is unlikely that he would possess enough money to fund DNA design himself—or that Tropicana had the facilities and specialists to perform such a monumental task).

After successful germination, Valisk grew at the same rate as any standard Edenist habitat. Rubra loaded the neural strata with a modified version of the standard initializing thought routines (again rumored to be a pirate copy of Edenist routines). From its maturation onwards, the habitat served as a base for his starship fleet, and for various industrial stations. Curiously, no attempt was ever made to mine He_3 from the gas giant. Again it is speculated that Rubra was distancing himself deliberately from the activities of his earlier culture.

Valisk became a corporate state, existing primarily to endorse and support Magellanic Itg. Rubra wrote a very loose constitution giving himself and his heirs the position of executive committee, with elected local councils and commerce association groups set up to advise the committee. This element of democracy was intended to comply with basic Confederation membership rules, thus qualifying as an independent state, and therefore ensuring a seat in the Confederation Assembly (Valisk only ever applied for observer status, which it still retains).

In practice the executive committee takes advice from no one, but runs the habitat in conjunction with the personality (see Rubra's Family, page 214) purely in order to benefit Magellanic Itg.

Although this newly grown Valisk was a financially advantageous location from which to run his ever-expanding fleet of starships, the habitat still needed to attract a base population in order to provide it with a viable civilization. Industrial companies establishing locally registered stations were therefore granted weapons and research licenses, which were extremely liberal. Valisk thus started to attract companies specializing in military hardware.

Rubra also opened the habitat to immigration by "people who seek cultural and religious freedom," once more thumbing his nose at his own formal Edenist upbringing. This invitation attracted several fringe religious groups and alternative-lifestyle tribes, who believed that a bitek environment would provide them with free food from the starscraper glands and so enable them to avoid work. Over 9,000 of these people arrived over the course of the habitat's first twenty-five years, many of them drug- or stimulant-program addicts.

After tolerating their excesses throughout this period, Rubra's patience with them finally ran out. Fed up with their basically parasitical nature, he banned any more of them from entering. Those that remained on Valisk chose an "earthbound" experience, and lived in the park rather than in the starscrapers. They amalgamated over the next fifty years into the Starbridge community, adopting an extremely primitive lifestyle and religious beliefs extrinsic to all of the main creeds, but involving tarot, the psychic, astrology, numerology, etc.

Today there are approximately 25,000 residents living in various nomad caravans throughout the interior, rejecting technology entirely (though not averse to using medical nanonic packages, especially for childbirth). They continue to eat the food provided by the habitat glands, and work at their handicrafts to provide fundamental essentials, many being proficient carpenters and potters, and even jewelers. They salvage scrap metal and tend animal herds, as well as growing their own opium. Some of their handicrafts, especially woven rugs, are sold to tourists or even to visiting starship crews for sale across the Confederation.

Even within the Starbridge community there is considerable division. Some actively embrace their existence and contribute a great deal to their community, while a minority are little more than wasted stimulant junkies.

By 2330, Valisk's population had risen to 350,000. Industrial output was high, with nineteen stations, a large spaceport, and many interstellar companies opening offices there; so the habitat became a financially viable proposition. Magellanic Itg by now had over 200 civil-cargo starships and 100 interplanetary craft.

It is at this time that the first blackhawks appeared, which were Rubra's second successful venture in covertly acquiring and subverting Edenist technology. The first ones to gestate in Opuntia's rings were registered with Magellanic Itg, and were captained by Rubra's children (see Rubra's Family, page 214). They swiftly replaced the Magellanic line's ZTT starships, and to this day they form Magellanic Itg's entire fleet, although not all its captains are descendants of Rubra himself.

Rubra died in 2390, by which time he had become one of the wealthiest men in the Confederation. Magellanic Itg had industrial concerns in fifty star systems, and a fleet of 500-plus blackhawks, as well as financial interests in stock markets on several hundred worlds. However, while it would be unfair to say the company and habitat have declined since then, they have certainly never again emulated that initial period of dynamic growth. This is mostly part due to the inheritance problems Rubra left behind him (see Rubra's Family, page 214).

Today the habitat's reputation is in almost complete disrepute. Magellanic Itg has increasingly contracted around its core businesses of interstellar transport and operating manufacturing stations in nearby star systems. The habitat's attendant stations are now almost totally given over to the production of armaments. The executive committee, composed of Rubra's descendants, is prone to power struggles, exasperated by the habitat personality, which invariably weaken the company's commercial edge.

In the last century there have been two notable attempts by the executive committee to regain the company's earlier prestige. First was the Von Neumann machine (started in 2508, main section completed in 2521), a combination of bitek and nanocybernetics, which is positioned 50km from Valisk. This machine was only partially successful. Its main problem was its inability to reproduce itself without subsystems supplied by an outside manufacturing capability. It is too complicated in its present form, although much information regarding self-replication technology has been learned from its construction. It remains operational, and is still capable of producing a considerable amount of finished products, notably heavy structures such as spaceport and industrial station sections.

As part of an ongoing research and development project, company scientists are continuing to refine and upgrade its cybernetics and software. Unfortunately, the executive committee now allocates few funds to this once-prestigious project, and further development is slow. Should a positive leader gain control of the executive committee, a second-generation machine may be constructed.

The second attempt is the Portal project. This has absorbed a great deal of the company's financial resources over the last seventy years. The idea is to open wormholes on a permanent basis, providing interstellar transit to relatively unsophisticated (cheap) ships, thus reducing travel costs considerably. It may even be possible to have ordinary spaceplanes use planet-orbiting portals, eliminating the need for both starships and interplanetary craft. Although most industrial star systems (and the Edenists) have projects running on similar lines, none has put quite so much effort into the concept as Magellanic Itg. If it proves successful it will be as revolutionary as the first FTL ship, and give the company enormous status and financial rewards.

Rubra's Family

When he died Rubra was known to have fathered over 150 children, of whom eighty-five were gestated in exowombs from ova he had bought. All the exowomb born had modifications made to their affinity gene, as well as general physiological improvements. The thirty which Rubra considered the most promising were appointed to Valisk's executive committee, while the remainder—and also several of the next generation—became blackhawk pilots. His naturally conceived children were virtually disinherited from the company, and many of them returned to the Edenist fold.

Under normal circumstances this executive committee arrangement should have been capable of furthering the company growth in spectacular terms, providing a Edenist type of consensus governing body. However, Rubra had his exowomb children's affinity gene modified in such a way that they were affinity-bonded only with Valisk, and with the first family of blackhawks. They did not share the Edenist unity, and were controlled to an extensive degree by the habitat personality.

Rubra, when he died, transferred his personality pattern to the habitat, and extended its template into every existing thought routine. From this position he still attempts to run Valisk and Magellanic Itg as if he were a living human. Certainly his children are dominated to a large extent by his wishes and his influence, because the habitat personality has access to their thoughts virtually from the moment of conception, and makes considerable use of this link in shaping their thought processes. This is a gross breach of Edenist ethics, and remains the mainstay of Edenist opposition to both Valisk and Magellanic Itg.

In effect, Rubra's descendants are therefore little more than stunted puppets under the influence of his personality pattern. Very few have ever managed to break free from Valisk, not through any physical restraints but because the psychological prohibition is too great.

The habitat will not accept personality patterns from any other people that die, so it remains entirely Rubra's domain. Edenists claim that he/it is not sane, and few of them ever visit Valisk. Edenists will not even purchase any goods produced in Magellanic Itg industrial stations, nor is there a branch office of the Jovian Bank on Valisk (making it one of the very few exceptions in the Confederation).

It is estimated that there are well over 1,000 of Rubra's descendants who now contain this restrictive affinity gene, and thus fall under the personality's domination. The executive committee accounts for thirty of them; blackhawk captains make up another 300; and a further 250-plus hold managerial posts throughout Magellanic Itg. The rest continue to live in Valisk, but some have dropped out and joined the Starbridge community, while others are employed by the Magellanic Itg company in minor roles.

Five

Sentient Xenoc Species

1. Tyrathca

A. From Pre-2611 Information

The Tyrathca were discovered in 2395 on Hesperi-LN, a planet 227 light-years from Earth. They are not indigenous, since their home planet, Mastrit-PJ, is on the other side of the Orion Nebula, and not visible from the Confederation. According to the Tyrathca themselves, their sun expanded into a red supergiant 14,500 years ago. Breeder pairs left the star system on several hundred slower-than-light arkships (the exact number is unknown), 15,000 years ago. These arkships were hollowed-out asteroids capable of reaching 15 percent lightspeed. Their aim was to establish as many Tyrathca colonies as possible. It is not known how many colonies were actually established, but the arkship Tanjuntic-RI, which founded the Hesperi-LN colony, had stopped in at least five other systems to land breeder pairs on Tyrathca-compatible planets, and had examined some thirty further star systems via remote probes.

Hesperi-LN was the last colony established by Tanjuntic-RI. After 13,000 years in flight, and despite constant refurbishment and resupply in the star systems it examined, the arkship had reached the end of its useful lifetime, and Hesperi-LN was established in AD 1300.

Taking the flight of 300 arkships which left Mastrit-PJ into account, and assuming each of them was as successful as Tanjuntic-RI in locating new planets, the Tyrathca race may now be spread throughout a sphere of space at least 4,200 light-years in diameter, with perhaps as many as 1,500 colony worlds. Since acquiring human FTL technology, the Hesperi-LN colony has not bothered to contact any other sibling colony (see Psychology, page 226), a situation which both human and other xenoc members of the Confederation are quietly content with. They evidently evolved quite late in Mastrit-PJ's geological history. It may be that their planet possessed a Venus-type reducing atmosphere for several billion years, which didn't alter until the sun began to cool. Records of their history are very fragmented, and they show no real interest in their own past (see Psychology, page 226).

Arkship Technology

The arkships employed fusion drive, with a deuterium reaction used to accelerate the vehicle up to 15 percent lightspeed. Three separate biosphere chambers were built in each arkship, each of them with independent systems in case of an accident.

The Tyrathca controlled their breeding on board, so that no stress was ever placed on the ships' internal resources. Arkships carried a maximum of 25,000 breeder pairs, with as many as 60,000 members of the vassal caste. The arkship fleet was equipped with communication lasers, which were used regularly in the first 2,000 years of the exodus, exchanging technical and planetology data. After this, the fleet became so dispersed that communication between ships began to fall off. Today it has ceased altogether.

Tyrathca Physiology (Breeding Pairs)

The Tyrathca have a standard biochemical arrangement: their cells contain organelles and a nucleus, and their DNA is a double helix; they digest protein for energy, and they breathe oxygen. They possess a large number of organs with varying filtering and corpuscular production functions, giving a Tyrathca a highly complex internal layout.

The Tyrathca has an ochre-colored hide which, although harder than animal skin, is not quite an exoskeleton; it is quite similar to scales, but also very flexible. A coating of dry ochre-gold dust, similar to a terrestrial moth, is exuded from this hide, leaving sprinklings of it wherever the Tyrathca walks. Its main body is horizontal, 2m long, with four legs that keep the underbelly 1.4m above ground level, and a tapering, meter-long neck which curves up towards the vertical.

The head is a 50cm-high egg shape, tilted backwards at about 10°. It has a flattish face with a broad mouth at the bottom, and two eyes but no nose, all its breathing being done through the mouth, and the olfactory receptors double as tastebuds. The mouth has a double-lip arrangement; each segment is solid, so the lips are not flexible like human lips. The first (outer) set of visor-like lips part for breathing, the second (inner) lips open for eating, so the first pair are constantly in motion. The scaly hide covering the rest of the head is slightly furry. The crest of the head rises 2.9m above the ground.

The Tyrathcas' method of communication is vocal, consisting of high-pitched whistles. These are produced in a tubular pipelike organ located between the two jaws, through which air is expelled from the lungs. This whistling is very fast and complex, and while a Tyrathca cannot make human vocal sounds, humans cannot reproduce the Tyrathcas' whistle either, so all interspecies communication needs to be conducted through an electronic interpreter. On either side of the neck, just below the head itself, there are two small teats with the vassal-caste chemical program secretion glands behind them. Both male and female breeder Tyrathca possess these.

A spine ridge runs down the back of the neck and along the center of the torso to the rump, and it sprouts hair in a similar fashion to a mane, This hair can be brown, ochre, rust-red or black. Aside from the four legs, there are two arm-analogue limbs extending from the base of the neck, where it merges with the body. These arms are thin but stronger than their human equivalent, and they have one elbow joint, which can hinge at almost 200°. Each hand is completely circular, with nine fingers spaced equidistantly around it. The "wrist" joint connects to the middle of one side of this hand, and consists mainly of a gristly physical structure which can bend and twist in every direction.

Above but slightly behind the shoulders for each arm are two back-trailing extrusions resembling whip antennae. They are 9cm in diameter at their base, tapering to a rounded tip, and 1.5m in length. These appear to be vestigial tail-analogues used for maintaining balance when the Tyrathca were in their pre-sentient form (several of the vassal-caste species still possess functional antennae).

Tyrathca legs have a single knee and, like the arms, seem thin in relation to the body bulk. The front pair of legs have nine small toes. On the rear pair, the toes on each foot have merged into a single, flap-like unit at the front, to allow for an easier grip on uneven surfaces. Tyrathca cannot use human-style stairs, so all their own buildings employ spiral ramps.

Externally, the males and females are almost identical. However, the males' antennae tend to be longer, while females are marginally larger in body, to accommodate their complex ovary arrangement.

Technically the Tyrathca are mammalian, although they do lay eggs. The breeder pairs are always omnivores, though vassal castes include omnivore, herbivore and carnivore species. They cannot survive cold climates, becoming sluggish and confused when the temperature approaches freezing; exposure to −5°C will kill them. They can function normally in temperatures up to 45°C, though their preferred median is 35°C. The Tyrathca evolved in a 0.87 gravity field, and find the normal human standard slightly uncomfortable. However, they will colonize a planet with up to a 0.94 gravity field. High-acceleration spaceship travel is dangerous for them, since their complex internal organs are susceptible to membrane tearing in a high-gee field. Tyrathca life expectancy is forty-five years, and maturity (in breeders) is reached three to five years after hatching.

The breeders will sleep for up to ten hours during the night. Mastrit-PJ's day was twenty-eight hours, so they cannot adjust to a planet having a day shorter than twenty hours.

Tyrathca do not suffer a long period of old age. The onset of senescence is swift, and this phase lasts for no more than two months, the symptoms being memory loss and lack of coordination. Once it is established beyond any doubt, a breeder will simply retreat into its house and stop eating. The breeder it has been paired with will accompany it for its demise, though this is a cultural tradition rather than any physiological necessity. Breeding pairs tend to be of roughly similar age.

The Tyrathca have never performed genetic modifications on themselves, nor have they expressed any interest in it when the Confederation has offered this technology to them. They regard their inherent form and life expectancy as completely adequate.

Vassal-Caste Genealogy

The dominant Tyrathca are, of course, the breeders, these being the only fully sentient type and the only one able to reproduce. There are six species of the vassal caste, each with its own specialized functions. Although their arrangements are similar to those seen in an insect hive hierarchy, the Tyrathca are not in fact evolved from insects. This is simply the result of social specialization during pre-sentient times, when lower clan/herd members performed the tasks assigned to them by the buck/chieftain. The Tyrathca did spend a very long time (800,000 years) in their pre-sentient form (human Neanderthal-equivalents), allowing a complete development of this social system.

The vassal castes are as follows:

Builder
Larger than the breeder, slow moving but very strong. Its mouth is used to chew soil, adding chemicals to produce a cement which is used to construct buildings. A herbivore, it lives for twelve years.

Farmer
Small (dog-sized), it tends crops and is capable of other light work. Also a herbivore, it will live for eight years.

Hunter
Medium-sized, with no forward arms, though a vestigial bone structure remains. It can move extremely fast, and has horns at the base of its long snout. It chases and kills its prey. Its balance antennae are longer than its body, and fully active, and the front legs have paws with long sharp talons. A carnivore, it lives for ten years.

Housekeeper

Similar in appearance to the farmer, but with greater memory capacity. This vassal will keep the breeders' home tidy, serve them in simple tasks, and nurse the vassal-caste hatchlings. An omnivore, it lives for eight years.

Tree Scavenger

Another small species, and the most lively, its behavior rather similar to a terrestrial kitten. It is very agile, and able to climb trees and rock cliffs. Since the farmer type is unable to climb, this one was probably in primitive times intended as a fruit picker. A herbivore, it survives for five years.

Soldier

Large, and almost the same size as a breeder, which it closely resembles. It is also the most intelligent of the vassal castes, and is quite capable of using high-technology weapons as readily as spears and clubs. It will instinctively defend all members of the breeder pair's family, giving priority attention to their young—the future breeders. It possesses an instinctive grasp of tactics, enabling a pack of "soldiers" to operate very effectively together. It lives for a good fifteen years.

All the vassal species will readily accept verbal orders from the breeders they serve. However, except in the case of the soldiers, these comprise simple stop–start orders. Instead, more intricate instructions on how to perform complex tasks (such as the best way to catch a specific prey, design a building, or catalogue edible plants) must be loaded into these vassals via a chemical program that is secreted by the breeders' neck teats. The synthesis of these chemicals is fast and extraordinarily complex. A breeder will literally think out a sequence of movements—or picture a certain shape—and the gland will start building this thought pattern into a chain of molecules, which is then absorbed by the vassal. Once an instruction of this kind has been chemically implanted, it can subsequently be activated by a brief verbal command at any time throughout that same vassal's life. The bundle of nerve fibers connecting the teat synthesis glands to the breeder's brain is as thick as its spinal cord.

Reproduction

The female breeders undergo two reproduction cycles, one for producing the vassal castes, the other for producing new breeders, and they occur fifteen months apart.

During the vassal egg fertility cycle, which lasts for two months, the female ovaries will produce eggs in a distinct sequence: 1. Soldier, 2. Builder, 3. Tree scavenger, 4. Hunter, 5. Housekeeper, 6. Farmer.

The female breeder always knows the fertile period for each egg sequence, so the breeders can easily select the vassals they most urgently require, but four to six eggs for each caste are the normal choice during one fertility cycle.

The breeder egg cycle is shorter, at three weeks. As many as eight eggs will be produced, and always in male–female pairs. Mated couples will always choose exactly how many breeder offspring to produce, dependent on their current economic or social circumstances—a tradition which proved useful when they lived in confined conditions on the arkships. Tyrathca do not experience orgasm, which takes the more basic kind of instinct out of their mating, so their egg-laying is instead dictated by logical requirements.

Fertilized eggs are ejected from the female's body after three days. These are hard when they emerge, and will hatch after fifteen to twenty days, depending on their type. Their eggs are more definitely spherical than any terrestrial eggs, with only a slightly ovoid shape. Egg size varies from 25cm for a tree scavenger, up to 90cm for a builder; breeder eggs are 60cm. Their eggs do not require brooding, yet must be kept reasonably warm. Tyrathca living in technology-based cultures use electrically heated blankets for this purpose. The agricultural/pastoral Tyrathca (such as the Lalonde farmers) set their eggs on some rock which will receive plenty of sunlight, and in traditional homes they are placed up on the roof, which catches the most sun and can be more readily defended.

Psychology

In human terms, the Tyrathca are incredibly phlegmatic. They have never demonstrated any innovative flair, and appear to completely lack imagination. It is a constant puzzle to human researchers how they ever developed any kind of industry, let alone the technology required for interstellar flight. Once settled on Hesperi-LN, they showed no inclination to build another arkship or continue their colonization efforts. Tanjuntic-RI was simply abandoned (the Tyrathca commercial council granted human researchers permission to explore it, but could not understand their interest in it).

Their major emotional responses seem to be directed towards their (breeder) offspring, of which they are fiercely protective. However, as long as the world or society into which these youngsters are released seems stable, they are perfectly content. A secondary emotion is the bond of each breeder Tyrathca with its partner; they mate for life, and if one dies the other effectively loses the will to live, duplicating the mutual withdrawal behavior they practice at the onset of old age.

In their immature state the Tyrathca display an almost human range of emotional responses, being excitable, enthusiastic and argumentative like human children. But this stage of behavior is rapidly abandoned as they approach their third year.

On reaching maturity, Tyrathca breeders leave their homes in search of a mate and a community they will find acceptable. These communities are all single-stream: one may specialize in chemistry, while another may produce agricultural machinery, and so on. Once both a mate and a suitable location have been found, the new pair will continue living there for their lifetime.

Religion
They have none.

Education

This is received via the chemical-program glands. A parent will provide what can be termed a basic literacy chemical program for its offspring, consisting of language, mathematics, local geography and animal and plant life, information on how to operate household appliances, etc. After adulthood is reached, a Tyrathca will travel until it finds an area practicing the profession which interests it (it may well stay in its home town), and once it has found a like-minded mate, they will set up a home and acquire specialist knowledge from an adult working in their chosen profession. This knowledge also comes in the form of a chemical program.

So a Tyrathca coming to a profession will start work with a store of information that has taken centuries to acquire. This seems to be nature's equivalent to Adamist didactic imprints and Edenist educational affinity. Although this system ensures that knowledge is generally area-specific, there are some fields which are homogeneous, such as medicine and basic engineering (a local repair and service operation).

Technology

As a species, their technological level is high, although the Tyrathca do not always exploit the most advanced systems available to them. Their philosophy is very much one of appropriate application; a farming community will not use fusion generators to power its machinery, as in their view this would require a whole new field of specialization not possessing any crossover into other fields of activity beneficial to them.

They still retain all the technical expertise they acquired from building and maintaining Tanjuntic-RI. Several of these fields had undergone devolution by the time contact began with the Confederation, but only in terms of practical usage. The most prominent of these was advanced computer science. Although it was essential for interstellar flight, only a mediocre level is required for on-planet use, such as communications and industrial systems, therefore only a mediocre level of it was being manufactured. Most puzzling to humans was the fact that when it was obvious that only advanced-level computer systems would be acceptable for selling exports and gaining foreign currency, the Tyrathca communities that produced computers were making these advanced systems within five years. Their knowledge of how to build such items was still intact, and being passed down through the generations, but it was just not required.

Hesperi-LN has a telecommunications network (integrated local systems), but no equivalent of the human entertainment media. There is a road network, although it is maintained by local governments, so its quality varies accordingly. Aircraft are built by only two communities, and both marques fall into the emergency services class. There are no passenger airlines, nor is there any analogue to tourism. Some ocean-going ships exist, but trade between continents centers on mineral exchange, and it is relatively small. Ships also service the platforms housing ocean thermal generators (see Power Sources, page 231).

Economy

This operates very differently from the human concept. The Tyrathca use a global accounting system rather than a currency. Existence of the vassal castes means that there is little trade in basic foodstuffs. The agrarian communities tend to specialize in foods particularly suited to local environmental conditions.

Although there is a multitude of each kind of specialist-hardware production centers, they do not compete against each other. For example, an engineering factory will distribute its products only over its own allocated area, whose boundaries are defined by transportation costs. A boundary will lie exactly halfway between two engineering factories (taking difficult terrain into account), and every community on either side of that boundary will always go to its own central factory for its engineering requirements. As the Tyrathca always share their knowledge amongst themselves, their level of standardization is total and complete in every discipline.

Since contact began with the Confederation, a new specialization of merchant has been evolved, responsible for earning foreign currency. Confederation currency is required principally to hire starships in order to establish new Tyrathca colonies and trade in those very few commodities they lack internally, or particularly value.

A space-based industry is starting to develop in the Hesperi-LN star system. Before contact with the Confederation, the Tyrathca had eight industrial asteroid communities spread throughout the Hesperi-LN system, producing basic microgee compounds for the planet. Subsequently, two asteroids have been shifted into high planetary orbit, and development of new free-fall industrial techniques has started (the Tyrathca either never wanted asteroids in orbit around their planet, or never thought up the concept). Production under license has begun of components from human astronautics companies, and eventually indigenous FTL starship design is expected. It does seem to take the Tyrathca a very long time to learn anything new, which is why their industry expands so slowly. However, once they have mastered the art of a new concept, complete understanding of it is spread rapidly and easily through their bodily chemical programs.

The general level of technology on Hesperi-LN has risen perceptibly since contact began with the Confederation.

Power Sources

Hesperi-LN employs hydroelectric dams and ocean thermal exchange generators to provide power. There are no fusion generators, even though the Edenists have expressed a willingness to supply them with He_3. The existing renewable sources are quite sufficient for all Tyrathca requirements.

Government

The nearest human equivalent of the Tyrathca system would be federalization. Governance, if it can truly be said even to exist, is very localized. The different areas organize themselves with very little debate, arranging civil organizations such as the ambulance service or telecommunications very much to suit themselves. There is no voting or elections, since all Tyrathca automatically work for the common purpose. Crime and personal advancement to the detriment of others are not concepts which they even understand, let alone practice.

If something like a road needs building, then all involved will simply discuss what is required, and then get on with it. The main problem with this, from other Confederation traders' viewpoints, is their lack of distribution networks or their understanding of the needs of outsider communities living among them—or even getting to know about such needs. The new Tyrathca merchant communities have worked hard to develop computerized inventories to minimize this cultural gulf with outsiders, and to send representatives across the planet to locate markets able to provide imported goods for their alien residents.

It is these same merchant communities, established around the various spaceports, which have become the most authoritative voice speaking for the Tyrathca when it comes to relations with the Confederation, principally because they are the ones who bring in Confederation money for the fellow members of their race.

The Tyrathca have only four offplanet embassies: on Avon for the Confederation Assembly, on the Kulu Kingdom, on Jupiter, and on Earth (though actually based in the O'Neill Halo, where their preferred gravity level can be more closely matched). An ambassador breeder-pair family will assume this role for their lifetime, and they pass on to their offspring an understanding of human culture through their programming chemicals, so they in turn can carry on the same profession. Tyrathca embassies also act as merchant agents for Hesperi-LN.

The merchant communities have formed a central economic council to deal with large projects such as funding colonies and developing asteroid settlements.

The Confederation has appointed a special commissioner to oversee all Tyrathca contacts with humans, who acts to prevent them from being exploited. All commercial contracts are subject to veto by this commissioner's office.

Buildings

All Tyrathca houses follow the same traditional layout: a cylindrical tower, tapering upwards slightly, which can accommodate the spiral ramps they need, and rising four storys high. In the race's pre-technology phase these houses were made solely of stone and mud cement (see Builder, page 223). However, they are now constructed of cut stone, bricks, wood, composite, etc., depending on the nature of the particular community and what materials are locally available. Modern conveniences such as electric lights, cookers, telecommunication links, heaters, plumbing, etc., are now included, of course. It is still the builder caste who do all the necessary manual labor and, once loaded with the appropriate chemical program, they are now as capable of handling modern materials as they were stone and mud. The doors are always arched, and the windows round, while arches are used to support the interior floors and ramps.

The Tyrathca have no other concept of architecture, although the sheer alien-ness of these towers makes them look impressive constructions to human visitors.

Their houses are only lived in for one generation, and this is true even for the houses of communities involved in the technological professions. For once a breeder pair reaches senescence, both they and their vassal-caste dependents will withdraw inside the house, and builders will proceed to seal them in. This inevitable conversion of houses into tombs causes an outward ripple effect in the towns. Thus the older a town is, the further out it will extend, as the abandoned area occupied by the dead eventually becomes larger than the peripheral area still inhabited by the living. After several generations, this outer, inhabited ring becomes so widely separated and far-flung (typically 15–20km from the original center) that it becomes impractical to sustain communications, and the surviving community then shifts en masse to a new location. This is the only occasion when a Tyrathca will move house, and it happens only once every few generations.

Public buildings, of which there are few, such as utility stations and factories, are strictly functional and do not follow the traditional tower shape. In fact their modern factories can look surprisingly similar to human structures. When a community needs to relocate, the production equipment from such a factory will be taken along with them (where practical), but the building itself remains. These abandoned towns are never revisited.

Defense

The defense of Hesperi-LN is managed by the Confederation Navy. There are twenty-five strategic-defense weapons platforms orbiting the planet, and a supporting sensor network.

Although there is very little of value to humans on this planet, or indeed within the entire star system, the Confederation remains concerned about the captains of rogue starships attempting to blackmail the Tyrathca with the threat of surface bombardment. Ever since the Tyrathca were first discovered, there have been rumors about mineral wealth on Hesperi-LN, which the Tyrathca have supposedly mined and stored. Although these are without foundation, the Assembly remains concerned about the prospect of unprovoked assaults, and therefore funds the local SD network.

The Tyrathca pay 5 percent towards the cost of their own defense. Some of the astroengineering companies transferring industrial technology to them have been approached by the merchant council to sun-license the production of combat wasps. This request is currently under negotiation with the Assembly-appointed commissioner. As an officially equal partner in the Confederation, there is no legal reason why the Tyrathca should not be given full access to human weapons technology. However, most member-state governments have deep reservations about handing over such powerful technology to a species whose past was once violent enough to develop a soldier caste.

B. From Post–2611 Information

Mastrit-PJ

The Tyrathca home system is 2,300 light-years from Earth, hidden behind the Orion Nebula (itself 1,500 light-years away from Earth), which extends thirty light-years across.

Mastrit-PJ's star expanded into a red supergiant 14,500 years ago, with a radius of 420m km in diameter, engulfing all the planets which originally orbited it.

Early History

One of three sentient races to evolve on Mastrit-PJ, the Tyrathca were in fact the last to achieve sentience.

Ridbat

The first species to evolve were the Ridbat, whose civilization flourished a million years ago. They were smaller than the Tyrathca, with a flattened ovoid body, 1m high, 1.3m in diameter, and had four legs and four arms emerging in pairs on opposite sides of the body. There was a slim neck at the upper center of the body, with a rounded, wedge-shaped head and two large eyes allowing 300° vision.

The Ridbat eventually developed a high-technology civilization, establishing colonies on several moons and planets in the system. Although one attempt was made to bioform a Mars-like world, the project was never completed. All their other colonies were either domed or underground.

The Ridbat were a very clan-orientated species,

which gave them a high aggression factor. Their various nations were engaged in near-constant disputes, two of which resulted in the use of nuclear weapons on the planetary surface.

The total duration of their civilization (measured since the point of emerging from the hunter-gatherer stage into the farmer-builder stage) was around 15,000 years, 9,000 of which were pre-industrial. Their internal wars delayed any industrial development considerably, the population being repeatedly culled by military action. As a consequence their planetary population never rose above 500,000,000.

Major (industrial-era) wars knocked their global technology base back from advanced electronic-cybernetic to basic electrical-mechanical on at least three separate occasions. Apart from the deployment of military spy satellites and orbital weapons platforms, spaceflight was limited. They only used interplanetary spaceflight during their third industrial era. This was a period lasting nearly 700 years, and the most prosperous they ever enjoyed. It ended with a nuclear war on the planet itself, and the destruction of its offworld colonies. The Ridbat never attempted interstellar flight.

Their fourth, and last, industrial era was ended by the release of several biological weapon agents which wiped them out, along with 70 percent of the animal life existing on the planet at that time.

Little else is known about them.

Mosdva

The Mosdva were the second sentient species to emerge, and they still survive. The Mosdva has a flexible body 2m long, with an oval cross-section 75cm deep at the center. There are six limbs, paired equidistantly along the body. The hide is composed of a variety of hard scales (similar to the Tyrathca themselves) and is dark brown in color. The head is pointed, with two eyes and a beak mouth, and the neck looks different from the rest of the body by reason of the heavy wrinkles, which provide it with increased flexibility. Each limb is 1.5m long, with a ball-and-socket "shoulder" joint allowing considerable range of movement. The first limb section is 1.2m long, ending in a "wrist" joint. The foot/wrist appendage itself is lengthy, possessing nine digits. The forward pair of limbs has evolved into highly dextrous hands, the middle pair can be used for either manipulation or locomotion, but the rear pair is exclusively for locomotion.

When upright, the Mosdva can squat on its hind limbs, using the tail-end of its body as a tripod base to ensure greater stability. It can also shuffle about awkwardly using only its hind limbs, but walking and running at normal speeds involve use of the middle limbs as well. For a really quick "sprint," the front pair of limbs is also brought into play.

When it comes to climbing rock faces or trees, the Mosdva show amazing agility and balance, apparently having no sense of giddiness or vertigo.

When the middle set of limbs act as hands, they are employed mainly for largely passive tasks such as holding an object steady, their dexterity being less than half that of the front limbs.

There are two sexes and they are egg-layers, like all of Mastrit-PJ's other animal species, although the Mosdva are also marsupial. Both males and females possess pouches to contain their eggs as they move about. Newly hatched Mosdva do not use this pouch, even though they become mobile immediately.

The Mosdva are herbivores, with a dual stomach arrangement. Because Mastrit-PJ's plants have a woody structure, the first stomach is used to break up the bulk of their food intake, while the second one extracts nutrients from the previously pulped-up hydrocarbons, thus acting as a pre-intestine. Teats on the Mosdva are linked directly to this nutrient-extraction stomach, to feed their young with a high-protein fluid. There is no terrestrial-style milk-producing gland behind this teat. Both males and females suckle the young, and the suckling lasts for the first ten days until the infant's first stomach is capable of initiating its own enzyme production.

The Mosdva were still at a Neanderthal stage of evolution when the Ridbat achieved full sentience. They were incapable of high-order speech, but able to perform simple repetitive tasks. Consequentially, the Mosdva's evolution was forced on them. On seeing what useful servants they made, the Ridbat essentially enslaved them. They were specially bred over thousands of years, in a program which principally concentrated on advancing their dexterity and smartness (as defined by the ability to obey complex instructions).

By the time of the Ridbats' extermination, the Mosdva had attained the IQ level of a smart ten-year-old human child. Although their population was also much reduced by the Ridbat war, they did at least survive the biological agents released.

After this their genetic evolution reverted to a more normal pace. Because the Ridbat had also bred them for passivity and obedience, their own civilization developed extremely slowly. The ruined planet, with its exhausted mineral resources and extensive radioactive deadlands, was not an environment conducive to sophisticated or technology-based cultures, and the Mosdva psychology suited this well. They were not a species of researchers and dreamers. Instead they became nomadic, roaming between any still-habitable areas of the planet. This period started with an interval of nuclear winter, and once recovered from that slipped into a natural ice age. It was only when the glaciers retreated and the planet's biota began to recover, roughly 500,000 years after the Ridbats' fourth-era war, that the Mosdva started to advance again.

700,000 years after the destruction of the Ridbat, the Mosdva achieved a modest level of industrialization. Because the planetary reserves of petrochemicals, coal and natural gas had been depleted, their technology was based solely around the concept of level sustainability. It was a benign goal, and helped to maintain their society's status quo. Manufacturing corporations and market-driven competition did not occur on Mastrit-PJ under the Mosdva.

Although their engineering was kept to the equivalent of late-Victorian machinery, they did make considerable progress in theoretical fields such as physics, astronomy, mathematics, and (bio-) chemistry. Any advanced developments were used only where "appropriate," so as to preserve the ideal of stability around which their nature and world revolved. Although they were not opposed to change, any change generated from within was extremely slow in arriving.

The one irreversible alteration to their environment, over which they had no control at all, was the evolution of the Tyrathca. The latter's sentience began to develop fully after the end of the last ice age. Originally herd creatures, they developed specialized vassal castes to help feed and protect their clans.

Although intelligent, the Tyrathca are not in any way imaginative. This aspect of intelligence might have evolved eventually, but in their case it did not need to. Sharing their world with a species as benevolent and advanced as the Mosdva meant that they constantly had access to high technology.

Unfortunately for the Mosdva, the Tyrathca were more aggressive and confrontational, a trait deriving from their herd instinct. With their ability to copy technology, their greater physical size and larger numbers, they swiftly became the dominant of the two species.

This situation could well have spelled extinction for the Mosdva, as their settlements were put under considerable pressure from Tyrathca expansion. Then the Mosdva astronomers discovered that their star was about to expand into a red supergiant.

The Stellar Expansion Era

Once they realized the disaster confronting their world in approximately 1,300 years' time, the Tyrathca produced and implemented a racial survival plan. It involved two stages.

The first and more difficult stage was the constructing of arkships so that at least some of the population could escape to the stars, thus guaranteeing their ultimate racial survival. With a population already reaching 1,000,000,000, total evacuation on these arkships was clearly impossible. Even with the entire planet's industry mobilized, they would never be able to build sufficient numbers of them. The Tyrathca spent the first hundred years of this period forcing the development of an extensive spaceflight and orbital manufacturing capability. And for the second time in their existence, the Mosdva were essentially enslaved. Their smaller bodies, greater dexterity, and higher intelligence made them perfect astronauts. It was Mosdva technical expertise which was adapted and utilized to capture asteroids and shunt them into orbit around Mastrit-PJ, where they were hollowed out and converted into arkships. The arkship building phase lasted for 700 years, in which time 1,037 of them were built and launched.

After this, secondly, with the star's growing instability wrecking the planet's fragile ecology, the massive space manufacturing capability was switched to adapting asteroids into habitats. The asteroids chosen were orbiting more than 250m km from the star, putting them outside the predicted expansion photosphere. As this operation was far simpler than changing asteroids into giant starships, over 7,000 were created in just 200 years. Unlike the arkships, which were immediately lost to the Tyrathca upon completion, building these habitats was a near exponential-growth process, as new habitats used their industrial capacity to prepare yet more asteroids.

By the thousand-year stage, Mastrit-PJ had become uninhabitable and was completely abandoned.

However, no Mosdva was ever transported on an arkship, which were used exclusively by the Tyrathca. As soon as they had finished building one arkship, the Mosdva construction crew was cleared out of it and moved on to building the next one.

However, the Mosdva could not be excluded from the asteroid habitats without recourse to a policy of genocide. So the Tyrathca tolerated their continued presence, knowing that their own numbers were expanding and necessitated an ongoing habitat-construction program. And with the exact conditions of this population expansion unknowable, they would need Mosdva technical ability to help adapt the habitats to the environment of the swollen sun.

The Post-Expansion Era

The star expanded into a red supergiant which engulfed all of the system's planets. At the time of this expansion, there were 7,500 habitats, all orbiting within 3° of the ecliptic plane. The number of unused asteroids orbiting outside the photosphere was reduced to about 25,000, of which only 800 were larger than 5km in diameter.

The new radiant heat levels (higher than predicted)

meant that larger thermal-dissipation systems had to be constructed for the habitats. As a consequence, the habitats became even more engineering-dependent, which began a gradual shift of political power. Only Tyrathca breeders were capable of any meaningful technological activity, making all but the builder, housekeeper, and farmer vassal castes redundant. In habitats the soldier caste was bred solely to keep the Mosdva in line.

The revolution to overturn Tyrathca dominance occurred over a hundred-year period, starting 10,000 years ago. Post-expansion, the habitats initially formed a cohesive one-nation grouping. But the scarcity of raw matter, and competition for the remaining asteroids to mine, reduced the Tyrathca to outright competition between individual habitats. Wars were thus fought over the remaining inert asteroids, and each inhabited asteroid reverted to complete autonomy.

After that, the rise of the Mosdva to supremacy was inevitable. They controlled the habitat machinery and industrial facilities, a power which, as they discovered, enabled them to dictate their own terms to the Tyrathca.

This was the time when contact with the arkships broke down. Maintaining the interstellar communication lasers was purely a Tyrathca concern; with the end of their unified star-girdling society, so both the reason and capability declined. The last arkship messages were sent 9,300 years ago. And although some arkships probably kept on sending messages to the home system for some time after this, nobody there was listening.

The Mosdva Era

Even today not all habitats are under control of the Mosdva. At their peak, before the revolutionary millennium, there were approximately 13,000 Tyrathca habitat asteroids orbiting the red supergiant. Of these a mere 2,000-plus now remain under Tyrathca control. Most of the rest have banded together politically and physically under direct Mosdva dominion. Also, late expansion-era habitation concepts have adapted and evolved considerably from the original centrifugal-force gravity chambers.

The Mosdva with their climbing-adept limb arrangement are ideally suited to free fall, so have adapted extremely well to this environment. They no longer use rotating asteroids to live in. Such a use of mass was highly inefficient, most of the rock serving simply as a radiation and heat shield. Now they live in webs of tubing. These are huge disk-shaped structures, typically 8,000km in diameter, made up from a lacework of tube strands averaging 500m in diameter, although there is considerable disparity there. Each tube has a different function—habitation, food production, engineering, etc. They comprise sections linked together to form functional localized dominions which together make up the diskcity itself. The gaps between the tube strands are covered by reflective sheeting to prevent any light from penetrating to the far side.

Diskcities orbit mostly in the equatorial band, 10–15m km above the top of the photosphere.

Food for the Mosdva is mostly an alga or yeast grown in transparent piping in heavily foamed water.

This piping forms their recycling system, in a mechanical biological arrangement. Plants grown inside the tubes are often of edible varieties. Energy for general web functions is generated from the temperature difference between the sun-facing and the space-facing sides of the diskcity. The space-facing side is studded with heat fins of various designs, and even direct radiance projectors.

Dotted around the edge of the web are various chunks of captured mass, which are slowly being processed into raw chemicals for the industrial plants.

By angling the diskcity towards the sun's surface, it can be used like a sail, tacking to raise or lower its orbit and change its inclination—but only very slowly, such maneuvers taking several centuries.

Fusion generators are used mainly to turn hydrogen into nitrogen, the scarcest of all life-essential elements, as well as carbon and other elements. Hydrogen is sucked from the surface of the photosphere by ships with magnetic scoops.

In most webs there are knots and tangles. These tend to be the oldest parts, some still with Tyrathca settlements inside them. They started out being the original asteroids, which were tethered together, then their mass was progressively mined to produce the web tubes. Some of these sections are very ancient, and in disrepair.

The acquisition of new solid mass is now a slow process for the diskcities. Nearly all of the remaining outer asteroids have been captured. In pursuing their takeover policy, the Mosdva are now starting to physically assimilate the Tyrathca asteroid habitats. A diskcity can systematically pursue an independent asteroid, but takes centuries to perform the rendezvous. Eventually the two will collide, at which point the asteroid's mass is fed into the refineries, allowing the web to continue expanding. The diskcity usually destroys the target asteroid's heat-exchange systems several decades before the rendezvous, ensuring that there are no Tyrathca left alive when the asteroid is dismantled.

The independent Tyrathca asteroids have little defense against this process of absorption. Their asteroids possess few spaceships, and even fewer weapons, leaving them with little in the way of space-warfare technology. As it was always the Mosdva who piloted ships during the pre-expansion era, the breeders would now need to fly the ships themselves. Though they are more than capable of maintaining and flying spaceships (as the arkships prove), engaging in space warfare requires pilots with the kind of innovative mental agility which the Tyrathca simply do not possess.

Mosdva Society

Due to the difficulty in mining hydrogen, ships traveling between diskcities are mostly lightsail types, so in general there is little spaceflight. There is no trade between diskcities because that would involve losing precious mass from the disk itself.

A diskcity is typically divided up into several dominions, essentially separate nations which have constantly shifting alliances with other dominions. The inner dominions tend to be larger, with a high manufacturing capacity; while the outer dominions around the rim concentrate most of their effort on constructing and flying the scoopships. The raw mass which the ships carry back is then shipped to the inner dominions in exchange for finished products. All dominions retain enough industrial capacity to maintain their own life-support systems.

The Mosdva Language

The Tyrathca and Mosdva share a common language, although one that has seen several divergences between its use on asteroids, arkship colonies, and diskcities. The language is itself derived from the one formerly used by the Ridbat, and taught to early slave Mosdva. As the Tyrathca gradually acquired sentience, they naturally adopted the Mosdva language.

2. Kiint

A. From Pre–2611 Information

Jobis

The Kiint homeworld, Jobis, is 187 light-years from Earth, with an F2 star and 1.2 (Earth standard) gravity. It was discovered in 2356, and the Kiint race joined the Confederation in 2357. The Kiint are unique, out of all the technologically advanced xenoc species encountered so far by humans, in that they have no real interest in starflight (see Psychology, page 251).

Physiology

The Kiint are physically impressive, and are the largest sentient species in the Confederation. They are oxygen-breathers, with a standard biochemistry and cellular composition. Although the female gestates the fetus in her womb, they are not strictly mammals, and their blood temperature does not remain constant, but serves as a coolant fluid dissipating body heat through the hide.

They have been sentient for at least 200,000 years, and their organs and cells are highly evolved, with an efficiency several times greater than humans'. Part of their musculature is tractamorphic, with cells able to expand or contract, and in some cases twist. The Kiint body is 9–10m long, 3m broad, and covered by a white hide. It has eight legs, all equally thick and 2m long, resembling those of an elephant. Despite their bulk, their tractamorphic muscles give them considerable agility, so they can run swiftly, although they do not accelerate easily. The neck is inclined upwards to raise the crown of the head slightly above the main body.

The Kiint has a very wide face, with a central ridge dividing it into two planes. It has two eyes halfway up the face, and a series of six breathing vents are positioned below the eyes on either side of the central ridge, angled downwards, with furry fringes undulating constantly to act as dust and particle filters. The base (chin) of the head is slightly pointed, like a beak section for the mouth, and there are two other hinged beak sections behind it. The ears consist of long triangular membranes situated above and behind the eyes.

The Kiint's arms are tentacle-like appendages emerging at the base of the neck; composed almost entirely of tractamorphic muscle cords, they can assume a variety of shapes. Hand-analogues on the ends of these resemble large pods of flesh when inert, but are freeforming and able to produce fingers, suction cups, pincers, etc., within a considerable size range. This enables the Kiint to perform the most delicate kind of manipulation as well as feats of brute strength.

The Kiint are herbivores, and seem able to digest a wide range of xenoc plants. Because of their size, they generate a great deal of body heat, and so prefer a cool (temperate) climate. When working in tropical climates, they wear jackets woven with thermal-duct fibers to keep them cool. Jobis has a 1.2 gravity field, and a 27-hour day; the year is 420 (local) days long. The star is an F2 type.

The Kiint can adapt to terracompatible environments easily. Their life expectancy is unknown, since the Kiint are not forthcoming on such personal topics. They possess an ability similar to the Edenist affinity. This mode of communication has long since supplanted their voices, and they no longer retain the ability to make sounds. All Jobis animal life seems to participate in this Kiint affinity to some degree.

It is apparent that the flora and fauna of Jobis have undergone considerable modification. The planet's biosphere is remarkably benign. The animals are non-aggressive (though none of them has been raised to sentience), and the plants are mostly nutritional. To what degree the Kiint have modified themselves can only ever be speculative.

Psychology

The Kiint do display a recognizable emotional range, although all their responses seem milder than among their human equivalents. While they are undeniably more intelligent than humans, the Kiint do not possess the same curiosity about the physical universe—or at least they no longer display this characteristic. They have already achieved a level of technology exceeding that of humans (and also the Tyrathca), and have subsequently replaced scientific research with philosophical and cultural development.

Their sole interest in the Confederation seems to be in the opportunity it provides to them for observing other sentient entities, though the amount of actual observation which could be undertaken by the few ambassadors they have dispatched elsewhere must be very limited. This lack of curiosity about external affairs is perhaps best demonstrated by their absence of interest in starflight. The few Kiint ever to discuss the subject claim that they themselves experienced an extensive starflight era 130,000 years ago, but one they abandoned once they had reached their technological zenith. For once mastery of their physical environment was achieved, they saw no reason to explore the universe further, since all they ever encountered were variants on the same themes, in both life and cosmology.

The only time any Kiint have demonstrated any real enthusiasm for anything involving the Confederation was regarding the Laymil research project funded by the Lord of Ruin. Several Kiint are now assisting with the task of analyzing the Laymil race, and the instrumentation they have made available to the other researchers has proved invaluable. The Lord of Ruin does not make any payment to the Kiint involved in this project, as they participate simply because they desire to.

Although never gregarious, they can form friendships of a sort with humans, especially with individuals they regularly come into contact with.

Reproduction
This is another subject on which the Kiint are notoriously reticent. However, they do seem to practice monogamous relationships, though none has ever been observed mating. Duration of pregnancy is unknown, but given their large size is estimated at fifteen (Earth) months. Only one infant has ever been born inside the Confederation: Haile, the child of two researchers at Tranquillity.

Economy
Their economy is difficult to assess; in fact it is doubtful that the word "economy" as we understood it can even be applied. No manufacturing equipment has ever been seen on Jobis, but the Kiint seem to have mastered replication technology, though again this has never been demonstrated to humans.

Their house domes appear to provide all their everyday needs. What their non-everyday needs might be has never been ascertained.

The Planet Jobis

Jobis is a pleasant world (gravity apart), with extensive vegetation. Thanks to the Kiint's careful nurturing, most of its surface now resembles slightly wild parkland. There is no visible infrastructure of any kind, and the house domes are mostly gathered into small towns and villages, though a great many are also scattered at random over the rest of the land surface. There are none, however, to be found in the equatorial bands. These buildings enclose several partitioned areas separately dedicated to sleeping, eating and leisure, and they always possess a bathing pool. These house domes are built from many different substances, from ancient cut stone to modern composite.

There is no ground or sea transport system. All human visitors are required to land at a Confederation outpost, the small town called Urich, which comprises mainly embassies and trading company offices. The Kiint have provided this town with air capsules so that the humans there may travel around Jobis. These capsules are capable of traveling at extremely high speed (typically Mach 30), and accelerate at over 70 gees. The counter-acceleration force generated inside them leaves the occupants completely unaware of the flight. Yet no Kiint has ever been seen to use one of these capsules.

Kiint ambassadors always travel on human-manufactured starships, flying out in human spaceplanes or flyers to get aboard them. The CAB issues a special license for carrying Kiint passengers, which demands an extremely high standard of machine maintenance and flying proficiency.

The most startling aspect of the Jobis star system is the triad moons. These are three identical moonlets, measuring 1,800km in diameter, positioned at Jobis's Lagrange One point. Nothing about this formation appears natural, from their equidistant spacing to the actual composition of the moons themselves. They are composed of an aluminum silicon ore, and devoid of any geographical surface features. All the Kiint will say about them is that they were an old experiment.

Constant (passive) probing by human starships has revealed nothing to indicate the method of their formation/construction, nor what type of experiment they involved.

Government

The exact nature of their government is unknown. However, since the Kiint possess a type of affinity, their system is assumed to be similar to the Edenist consensus. When a Kiint ambassador speaks in any official capacity, he or she does so with total personal authority, and there is no referring back to Jobis for confirmation. The Edenists did once hope that this similarity would allow them to develop uniquely strong ties with the Kiint but, while relations between the Kiint and the Edenists are cordial, the Kiint take care not to demonstrate favoritism towards any Confederation faction in particular.

Trade

The Kiint show a large demand for human data, with emphasis on scientific papers and xenobiology reports. To purchase this they supply, in return, commercially valuable information to corporations and individuals. This information exchange is enough to provide an indicator to their own industrial past, as there seem few products regarding which the Kiint are unable to offer some suggestions for improvement. However, they will not supply any information on weapons, nor will they help initiate a completely new product or area of activity, but only upgrades for existing items and technology.

The Kiint undertake no trading with the Tyrathca. And, as far as is known, the Tyrathca merchant council has never approached Jobis with a view to trading either.

Communication

For conferring with Adamists, the Kiint use a vocalizer of their own manufacture, which speaks human languages fluently. When conversing with Edenists, they use affinity.

Defense

There are no visible defense mechanisms either on the planet itself or orbiting it, although the Confederation makes no attempt to downplay the errant-aggressive behavior patterns of its human members. There is a standard 100,000km exclusion zone in operation around Jobis, and spaceflight traffic is serviced by a human company.

It must be assumed, however, that any species capable of building the triad moons is fully capable of defending itself. Certainly no pirate has ever been rash enough to attempt an assault within the Jobis system.

Although Confederation Navy and national navy vessels are permitted in the Jobis system, the Kiint have requested that no military exercises be conducted within one light-year of their star.

The worst-case scenario, which the Confederation Assembly dreads, is that a pirate will one day attack some ship carrying a Kiint passenger. It is not known how the Kiint would react to the killing of one of their citizens, although realistically there seems little they could do about it. They are strong supporters of the overall policing-role concept of the Confederation, and obviously recognize the flaws of other species it contains.

B. From Post–2611 Information

It eventually became known that the actual Kiint homeworld is not even inside the Confederation galaxy. Jobis was simply a scientific outpost used to explore this galaxy.

The extent to which the Kiint had concealed their true abilities and culture from the Confederation is quite extraordinary. Hiding behind their claim of disinterest, they were able to promote the notion of their being a species concerned only with cerebral enhancement in a post-technological era. In fact they are—and all the time have been—very much at the height of their technological powers, having a teleport facility which does away with the need for starships, and they are actively and vigorously exploring this entire region of space. Their own homesystem does not have a single homeworld, but rather a ring of planets orbiting their sun (which is assumed to be their original sun). This system acts as a meeting point for all the sentient starfaring species in their galaxy (and presumably others), where knowledge and ideas can be exchanged.

That the Kiint are able to manufacture planets on such a scale is an indication of their awesome technical prowess, although the triad moons did hint at such an ability. As previously suspected, they have developed a perfect replicator to supply all their physical requirements.

Their government is referred to as the Corpus, which does seem analogous to the Edenist Consensus, although it is apparently more active and universal.

They have been observing the human race for at least 2,000 years. Humans with modified genes were specially bred to act as an observer team, and have been quietly watching and recording Earth's history for them. Apparently they followed the same policy for every other pre-spaceflight species, and observed many xenoc species in a similar fashion. Their non-intervention policy is enforced quite rigorously by the native observers.

Only two true humans, Joshua Calvert and Jay Hilton, have visited the Kiint homesystem. It seems that when the Confederation develops a stardrive capable of reaching their galaxy, humans will be permitted full access to the Kiint database.

3. Jiciro

This was the first sentient xenoc species to be discovered by the Confederation. A scoutship entered their system (180 light-years from Earth) in 2301.

At this time the Jiciro were a pre-technology civilization that was just moving into an agricultural age. It was therefore decided that no further contact should be made, so allowing the Jiciro society to develop without "contamination" by human concepts and technology.

The Confederation Navy maintains a station in the Jiciro system to ensure that no unauthorized starship flights are made to the planet. This station also houses a xenoc-monitoring team whose members are drawn from several participating universities. There are several sensor satellites in orbit above the Jiciro homeworld, and smaller spy systems disguised as local animals and insects roam the surface. This close-proximity observation will have to come to an end when the Jiciro reach a level of technical competence that would allow them to research such a monitoring device should they capture one.

As of 2611, some of their larger national groupings were beginning to experiment with the concept of steam-powered machinery.

Physiology
The Jiciro are bipedal hominids (a fact which caused a great deal of excitement at the time of discovery). Their average height is 1.5m, and they are thinner than terrestrial humans, possessing a different basic skeleton.

Their legs are shorter in proportion, and their arms emerge slightly further down the side of the torso. Their skin is a pale cream in color, and they have no facial or bodily hair. Their hands have seven fingers, each ending in a thick horn-like nail. Their facial arrangement is the same as a human's except for the nose, which is a horizontal gash above the mouth, with a bulbous lip below. The Jiciro have two tongues in their mouths, one on either side, and only a few teeth at the front, so they are limited to eating pulpy food. Their vocal range is wider than for humans, allowing them to produce high-frequency notes above human hearing capacity. Their life expectancy is ninety years.

Six

Principal Characters

A. The Main Protagonists

Joshua Calvert

Born in Tranquillity. His father, Marcus Calvert, was the owner and captain of the starship *Lady Macbeth*. Marcus died from organ failure due to substance and neural-stimulant abuse following a long term of depression after his last flight in the *Lady Macbeth*, during which the ship was damaged. Joshua was ten years old when Marcus died, and inherited his starship. His mother subsequently remarried.

Joshua has considerable geneering in his heritage, since the Calverts have been involved in the space industry for centuries, and have been modified accordingly. They do not suffer from free-fall sickness, and their bones and internal organs can withstand relatively high acceleration.

Joshua raised enough funds to repair the *Lady Macbeth* by scavenging the Ruin Ring for xenoc artifacts. The starship is now flown as an independent trader, traveling from system to system with commercial cargo.

Liol Calvert
Joshua's half-brother. Born in Ayacucho asteroid, in the Dorado system, he was conceived just before his father Marcus took *Lady Macbeth* on her last flight. Liol founded and has built up his own astroengineering company, Quantum Serendipity.

Ashly Hanson
Born in 2199, a one-way time traveler. At thirty years old he put his inheritance money in a trust fund managed by the Jovian Bank, which supplies him with long-term maintenance for a zero-tau pod. He remains in stasis for fifty years at a time, then spends five years looking around the Confederation before going back into stasis again. He is an excellent pilot, qualified for both atmospheric and spaceplane craft. A crew-member on *Lady Macbeth*.

Syrinx
Edenist captain of the voidhawk *Oenone*. She underwent a typical Edenist upbringing, although she was the most wilful of her ten siblings. This may be due to one of *Oenone*'s pattern energizers being the *Udat*, a blackhawk that would have a more liberal outlook than a voidhawk. Since a newly hatched voidhawk and its captain grow in physical symbosis for the first year, her personality would be forged in this time, and with that lingering influence.

She and *Oenone* took an early duty tour with the Confederation Navy, during which time she lost her brother Thetis and the *Graeae* during a mission to capture ships smuggling antimatter. After this time Syrinx became suspicious and mistrustful of Adamists in general.

Ione Saldana

The Lord of Ruin, a title which derives from her total command of the independent habitat Tranquillity. Technically the habitat is a duchy of the Kulu Kingdom, though in practice it has been an independent state since the abdication crisis of 2432.

As her embryo was brought out of zero-tau just when her biological father, Maurice, was dying, her only true "parent" is the habitat personality. They have an emotional bond remarkably similar to that of a voidhawk and its captain.

Rubra

Originally an Edenist Serpent, he germinated the independent habitat Valisk as a base for his company, Magellanic Itg. Upon his death, he transferred his personality into the habitat's neural strata, from where he continues to dominate his descendants. Regarded as mentally unstable by Edenists.

Dariat

An eighth-generation descendant of Rubra. Once considered the most promising of his generation by Rubra, he was quietly being groomed for leadership of Magellanic Itg through subtle psychological manipulation via affinity. When he was fourteen he fell in love with Anastasia Rigel, a member of the Starbridge tribe, who live inside Valisk. He killed a man he thought was a rival for her affections, and Anastasia subsequently committed suicide. Dariat erected an emotional block across his affinity link with the habitat, and refused to communicate with Rubra or his family ever again. He became a recluse for thirty years, plotting his revenge against Rubra, whom he held responsible for Anastasia's death.

Louise Kavanagh

Eldest daughter of Grant and Marjorie Kavanagh, and heiress to the Cricklade estate on Norfolk. As the wealthy provincial heir of an established landowning family, she was raised in considerable comfort. Educated as well as Norfolk and her class would permit, she is intelligent enough to question the political structure of her world. A keen horsewoman.

Quinn Dexter

A follower of the Light Bringer sect, he joined the coven in Edmonton as a teenager, coming directly under the influence of the High Magus, Banneth. No information exists on his life before this time. One of Banneth's favorites, and reasonably intelligent, he was promoted rapidly through the ranks, and became a devout believer in the Light Bringer.

Caught by Govcentral police carrying illegal nanonics into Edmonton, he was sentenced to Involuntary

Transportation and sent to Lalonde. On arrival at Lalonde, he was assigned to assist a group of pioneers, and was shipped upriver to a new settlement called Aberdale.

Gerald Skibbow

Married to Loren, with daughters Marie and Paula. A Govcentral civic worker, he lived in the Brussels arcology, but emigrated to Lalonde, bringing his family with him. They were upriver to Aberdale, and established a homestead for themselves on the nearby savannah, raising cattle.

Ralph Hiltch

Kulu ESA, a career agent, appointed head of station on Lalonde.

Dr. Alkad Mzu

Garrison national. A physics professor at the capital university, she moved to the Department of Defense when the Dorados settlement crisis with Omuta began to escalate. She developed the Alchemist, a doomsday weapon.

Laton

An Edenist Serpent, and one of the most feared people in modern history. Laton was rumored to be working on a proteanic virus capable of changing both the biological and psychological nature of humans, thus enabling him to subjugate entire planetary populations. When he began his first attempt to take over a habitat, Jantrit, the

Edenists and Confederation Navy sent a task force to stop him. He destroyed the habitat with antimatter, and fled with his co-conspirators. A space battle followed in which it was assumed he was destroyed. In reality, he escaped along with most of his group, and landed on Lalonde in the days before it was opened to colonization.

Samual Aleksandrovich

First Admiral of the Confederation Navy. A native of Kolomna, he relinquished its citizenship when he joined the navy as a career officer at twenty years old. He saw active service on several occasions, including Jantrit, before being promoted to command the 2nd Fleet.

B. Other Leading Figures

By Ship

Lady Macbeth

Melvyn Ducharme *Fusion specialist*
Sarha Mitcham *Systems specialist*
Dahybi Yadev *Node specialist*
Warlow *Cosmonik*
Beaulieu *Cosmonik*

Oenone

Ruben *Fusion systems*
Oxley *Pilot*

Cacus *Life support*
Edwin *Toroid systems*
Serina *Toroid systems*
Tyla *Cargo officer*

Villeneuve's Revenge
André Duchamp *Captain*
Desmond Lafoe *Fusion specialist*
Madeleine Collum *Node specialist*
Erick Thakrar *Systems specialist/CNIS undercover agent*

Udat
Meyer *Captain*
Cherri Barnes *Cargo officer*

Far Realm
Layia *Captain*
Furay *Pilot*
Endron *Systems specialist*
Tilia *Node specialist*

Arikara
Rear-Admiral Meredith Saldana *Squadron commander*
Lieutenant Grese *Squadron Intelligence Officer*
Lieutenant Rhoecus *Voidhawk Liaison Officer*
Kroeber *Commander*

Beezling
Kyle Prager *Captain*
Peter Adul *Alchemist team physicist*

Iles
Auster *Captain*

On Hellhawks
Rocio Condra *Mindori Possessor*
Cameron Leung *Zahan Possessor*
Etchells *Stryla Possessor*
Pran Soo *Varrad Possessor*

By Habitat

Tranquillity
Parker Higgens *Director, Laymil project*
Oski Katsura *Laymil Project, Electronics Division chief*
Kempster Getchell *Laymil Project astronomer*
Monica Foulkes *ESA agent*
Lady Tessa *ESA Head of Station*
Samuel *Edenist Intelligence agent*
Pauline Webb *CNIS agent*
Kelly Tirrel *Rover reporter*
Lieria *Kiint*
Nang *Kiint*
Haile *Juvenile Kiint*
Parris Vasilkovsky *Commercial cargo starship fleet owner*
Dominique Vasilkovsky *Parris's daughter, socialite*
Clement Vasilkovsky *Parris's son, university student*
Sam Neeves *Scavenger, pirate*
Octal Sipika *Scavenger, pirate*
Olsen Neale *Commander, Confederation Navy Bureau*

Valisk

Anastasia Rigel *Starbridge tribe member*
Kiera Salter *Marie Skibbow's possessor*
Stanyon *Possessor, Council member*
Bonney Lewin *Possessor, hunter*
Hudson Proctor *Possessor, Kiera's deputy, hellhawk liaison*
Tolton *Street poet, fugitive*
Tatiana Rigel *Fugitive*
Erentz *Rubra's descendant*
Dr. Ratan *Rubra's descendant, physicist*

By Asteroid

Trafalgar

Samuel Aleksandrovich *First Admiral, Confederation Navy*
Admiral Lalwani *CNIS Chief*
Captain Maynard Khanna *First Admiral's staff officer*
Admiral Motela Kolhammer *1st Fleet commander*
Dr. Gilmore *CNIS Research Division Director*
Jacqueline Couteur *Possessor*
Lieutenant Murphy Hewlett *Confederation Marine*
Captain al-Sahhaf *First Admiral's staff officer*

Koblat

Jed Hinton *Deadnight cult disciple*
Beth *Deadnight cult disciple*
Gari Hinton *Jed's sister*
Navar *Jed's half-sister*

Ayacucho

Ikela *Owner of T'Opingtu company and Garissan partisan leader*
Voi *Ikela's daughter*
Prince Lambert *Captain of the starship* Tekas
Dan Malindi *Partisan leader*
Kaliua Lamu *Partisan leader*
Feira Ile *Ayacucho SD commander, partisan leader*
Cabral *Media magnate, partisan leader*
Mrs. Nateghi *Lawyer*
Lodi Shalasha *Garissan radical*
Eriba *Garissan radical*
Kole *Socialite*
Shea *Prince Lambert's girlfriend*

Jesup

Lawrence Dillon *Light Bringer disciple*
Twelve-T *Gang lord*
Bonham *Light Bringer disciple*
Shemilt *Light Bringer disciple, SD commander*
Dwyer *Light Bringer disciple, systems specialist*

By Planet

Norfolk

Grant Kavanagh *Owner of Cricklade estate*
Marjorie Kavanagh *Grant's wife*
Genevieve Kavanagh *Marjorie and Grant's daughter*
Luca Comar *Grant Kavanagh's possessor*
Susannah *Marjorie Kavanagh's possessor*

Mrs. Charlsworth *Kavanagh sisters' nanny*
Mr. Butterworth *Cricklade estate manager*
Carmitha *Romany*
William Elphinstone *Trainee farm manager, Cricklade*
Fletcher Christian *Possessor*
Marcella Rye *Possessor, Colsterworth council officer*
Johan *Mr. Butterworth's possessor*
Celina Hewson *Louise's aunt*
Roberto Hewson *Louise's cousin*
Bruce Spanton *Marauder*
Véronique *Olive Fenchurch's possessor*
Kenneth Kavanagh *Merchant*

Lalonde
Powel Manani *IVET supervisor*
Lawrence Dillon *IVET*
Jackson Geal *IVET*
Ann *IVET*
Scott Williams *IVET*
Loren Skibbow *Colonist*
Marie Skibbow *Colonist, Gerald's daughter*
Paula Kava *Colonist, Gerald's daughter*
Ruth Hilton *Colonist, didactic imprint specialist*
Jay Hilton *Colonist, Ruth's daughter*
Father Horst Elwes *Colonist, priest*
Colin Rexrew *Governor*
Terrance Smith *Governor's executive aide*
Candace Elford *Chief Sheriff*
Lieutenant Commander Kelven Solanki *Confederation Navy*
Lori *Edenist Intelligence agent*

Darcy *Edenist Intelligence agent*
Maki Grutter *Lalonde Development Company employee*
Jenny Harris *ESA lieutenant*
Rai Molvi *Colonist, Aberdale council leader*
Rosemary Lambourne *Captain of the* Swithland
Karl Lambourne *Rosemary's son, crew-member of the* Swithland
Len Buchannan *Captain of the* Coogan
Gail Buchannan *Len's wife*
Laton *Serpent, in exile on Lalonde*
Camilla *Laton's daughter*
Yuri Wilkin *Deputy*
Mansing *Sheriff*
Graeme Nicholson *Rover reporter*
Lieutenant Murphy Hewlett *Confederation Navy Marine*
Reza Malin *Mercenary, team leader*
Pat Halahan *Mercenary*
Sewell *Mercenary*
Jalal *Mercenary*
Theo Connal *Mercenary, scout*
Sal Young *Mercenary*
Ariadne *Mercenary*
Shaun Wallace *Possessor*
Chas Paske *Mercenary*

Atlantis
Eysk *Fishing family chief*
Mosul *Eysk's son*

Ombey

Ralph Hiltch *ESA Head of Station, Lalonde, and General of the Liberation army*

Cathal Fitzgerald *Ralph's deputy*

Dean Folan *ESA G66 division*

Will Danza *ESA G66 division*

Kirsten Saldana *Princess of Ombey*

Roche Skark *ESA Director*

Jannike Dermot *ISA Director*

Landon McCullock *Police commissioner*

Diana Tiernan *Police Technology Division chief*

Admiral Farquar *Commander, Royal Navy, Ombey*

Captain Nelson Akroid *Armed Tactical Squad*

Finnuala O'Meara *Rover reporter, based in Exnall*

Hugh Rosler *DataAxis technician, Kiint observer*

Tim Beard *Rover reporter*

Neville Latham *Exnall's chief inspector*

Colonel Janne Palmer *Royal Marine*

Annette Ekelund *Possessor, Mortonridge defender*

Hoi Son *Possessor, Mortonridge defender*

Devlin *Possessor, Mortonridge defender*

Milne *Possessor, Mortonridge defender*

Sinon *Liberation army sergeant*

Choma *Liberation army sergeant*

Elena Duncan *Liberation army mercenary, boosted*

Dr. Riley Dobbs *Royal Navy personality debrief psychology expert*

Jansen Kovak *Royal Navy Medical Institute nurse*

Moyo *Possessor*

Stephanie Ash *Possessor*

Cochrane *Possessor*

Rana *Possessor*
Tina Sudol *Possessor*
McPhee *Possessor*
Franklin *Possessor*
Mixi Penrice *Petty criminal*

New California
Jezzibella *Mood Fantasy artist*
Leroy Octavius *Jezzibella's manager*
Libby *Jezzibella's dermal technology expert*
Al Capone *Brad Lovegrove's possessor*
Avram Harwood III *Mayor of San Angeles*
Emmet Mordden *Organization lieutenant*
Silvano Richmann *Organization lieutenant*
Mickey Pileggi *Organization lieutenant*
Patricia Mangano *Organization lieutenant*
Gus Remar *Rover reporter*
Lieutenant Commander Kingsley Pryor *Confederation Navy*
Webster Pryor *Kingsley's son, hostage*
Luigi Balsamo *Commander, Organization fleet*
Cameron Leung *Possessor of the blackhawk* Zahan
Oscar Kearn *Captain of the Organization frigate* Urschel
Bernhard Allsop *Possessor*

Kulu
Alastair II *The King*
Simon Blake, Duke of Salion *Chairman, Security Commission*
Lord Kelman Mountjoy *Foreign Office Minister*

Lady Phillipa Oshin *Prime Minister*
Admiral Lavaquar *Defense Chief*
Prince Howard *President of the Kulu Corporation*
Prince Noton *Ex-President of the Kulu Corporation*

Nyvan
Gelai *Possessor, Garissa genocide victim*
Ngong *Possessor, Garissa genocide victim*
Omain *Possessor, Garissa genocide victim*
Richard Keaton *Data security expert and Kiint observer*
Baranovich *Possessor, Organization sympathizer*
Adrian Redway *ESA Head of Station*

Earth
Banneth *Light Bringer in the sect of the High Magus of Edmonton*
Andy Behoo *Sellrat, Jude's eworld, London*
Ivanov Robson *Private detective, London*
Brent Roi *Detective, Halo police*
Courtney *Edmonton sect acolyte*
Billy-Joe *Edmonton sect acolyte*
Charles Filton-Asquith *West Europe supervisor, B7*

Others

The Confederation
Olton Haaker *Assembly President*
Jeeta Anwar *Chief presidential aide*
Mae Ortlieb *Presidential science aide*
Cayeaux *Edenist Ambassador*

Sir Maurice Hall *Kulu Kingdom Ambassador*
Rittagu-FHU *Tyrathca Ambassador*

The Kiint Home System
Tracy Dean *Observer*

The Edenists
Wing-Tsit Chong *Edenism's Founder*
Athene *Syrinx's mother*
Astor *Ambassador to the Kulu Kingdom*
Sinon *Syrinx's father*

The Mosdva
Quantook-LOU *Distributor of resources, dominion of Anthi-CL*

The Tyrathca
Baulona-PWM *Breeder, electronics regulator*
Waboto-YAU *Breeder, mediator for Coastuc-RT*

Seven

Timeline

2020	Clavius base established. Mining of Lunar sub-crustal resources starts.
2037	Beginning of large-scale geneering on humans; improvement to immunology system, eradication of appendix, organ efficiency increased.
2041	First deuterium-fueled fusion stations built, inefficient and expensive.
2044	Christian reunification.
2047	First asteroid capture mission. Beginning of Earth's O'Neill Halo.
2049	Quasi-sentient bitek animals employed as servitors.
2055	Jupiter mission.
2055	Lunar cities granted independence from founding companies.
2057	Ceres asteroid settlement founded.

2058 Affinity symbiont neurons developed by Wing-Tsit Chong, providing control over animals and bitek constructs.

2064 Multinational industrial consortium JSKP (Jovian Sky Power Corporation) begins mining Jupiter's atmosphere for He_3 using aerostat factories.

2064 Islamic secular unification.

2067 Fusion stations begin to use He_3 as fuel.

2069 Affinity bond gene spliced into human DNA.

2075 JSKP germinates Eden, a bitek habitat in orbit around Jupiter, with UN protectorate status.

2077 New Kong asteroid begins FTL stardrive research project.

2085 Eden opened for habitation.

2086 Habitat Pallas germinated in Jupiter orbit.

2090 Wing-Tsit Chong dies, and transfers his memories to Eden's neural strata. Start of Edenist culture. Eden and Pallas declare independence from UN. Launch buy-out of JSKP shares. Pope Eleanor excommunicates all Christians with affinity gene. Exodus of affinity-capable humans to Eden. Effective end of bitek industry on Earth.

2091 Lunar referendum to terraform Mars.

2094 Edenists begin exowomb breeding program coupled with extensive geneering improvement to embryos, tripling their population over a decade.

2103 Earth's national governments consolidate into Govcentral.

2103 Thoth base established on Mars.

2107 Govcentral jurisdiction extended to cover O'Neill Halo.

2115 First instantaneous translation by New Kong spaceship, Earth to Mars.

2118 Mission to Proxima Centauri.

2123 Terracompatible planet found at Ross 154.

2125 Ross 154 planet named Felicity, first multiethnic colonists arrive.

2125–2130 Four new terracompatible planets discovered. Multiethnic colonies founded.

2131 Edenists germinate Perseus in orbit around Ross 154 gas giant, begin He_3 mining.

2131–2205 One hundred and thirty terracompatible planets discovered. Massive starship-building program initiated in O'Neill Halo. Govcentral begins large-scale enforced outshipment of surplus population, rising to 2,000,000 a week in 2160: Great Dispersal. Civil conflict on some early multiethnic colonies. Individual Govcentral states sponsor ethnic-streaming colonies. Edenists expand their He_3 mining enterprise to every inhabited star system with a gas giant.

2139 Asteroid Braun impacts on Mars.

2180 First orbital tower built on Earth.

2205 Antimatter production station built in orbit around sun by Govcentral in an attempt to break the Edenist energy monopoly.

2208 First antimatter drive starships operational.

2210 Richard Saldana transports all of New Kong's

industrial facilities from the O'Neill Halo to an asteroid orbiting Kulu. He claims independence for the Kulu star system, founds Christian-only colony, and begins to mine He$_3$ from the system's gas giant.

2218   First voidhawk gestated, a bitek starship designed by Edenists.

2225   Establishment of one hundred voidhawk families. Habitats Romulus and Remus germinated in Saturn orbit to serve as voidhawk bases.

2232   Conflict at Jupiter's trailing Trojan asteroid cluster between Belt Alliance ships and an O'Neill Halo company hydrocarbon refinery. Antimatter used as a weapon; 27,000 people killed.

2238   Treaty of Deimos, outlawing production and use of antimatter in the Sol system, signed by Govcentral, Lunar nation, asteroid alliance, and Edenists. Antimatter stations abandoned and dismantled.

2240   Coronation of Gerrald Saldana as King of Kulu. Foundation of Saldana dynasty.

2267–2270   Eight separate skirmishes involving use of antimatter among colony worlds. 13,000,000 killed.

2271   Avon summit between all planetary leaders. Treaty of Avon, banning the manufacture and use of antimatter throughout inhabited space. Formation of Human Confederation to police agreement. Construction of Confederation Navy begins.

2300 Confederation expanded to include Edenists.

2301 First Contact. Jiciro race discovered, a pre-technology civilization. System quarantined by Confederation to avoid cultural contamination.

2310 First ice asteroid impact on Mars.

2330 First blackhawks gestated at Valisk, independent habitat.

2350 War between Novska and Hilversum. Novska bombed with antimatter. Confederation Navy prevents retaliatory strike against Hilversum.

2356 Kiint homeworld discovered.

2357 Kiint join Confederation as "observers."

2360 A voidhawk scout discovers Atlantis.

2371 Edenists colonize Atlantis.

2395 Tyrathca colony world discovered.

2402 Tyrathca join Confederation.

2420 Kulu scoutship discovers Ruin Ring.

2428 Bitek habitat Tranquillity germinated by Crown Prince Michael Saldana, orbiting above Ruin Ring.

2432 Prince Michael's son, Maurice, geneered with affinity. Kulu abdication crisis. Coronation of Lukas Saldana. Prince Michael exiled.

2550 Mars declared habitable by Terraforming office.

2580 Dorado asteroids discovered around Tunja, claimed by both Garissa and Omuta.

2581 Omuta mercenary fleet drops twelve antimatter planet-busters on Garissa, planet rendered uninhabitable. Confederation imposes thirty-year sanction against Omuta, prohibiting any interstellar trade or transport. Blockage enforced by Confederation Navy.

2582   Colony established on Lalonde.

PETER F. HAMILTON was born in Rutland, England, in 1960 and still lives near Rutland Water. He began writing in 1987 and has published short stories in a number of magazines and anthologies. His books include *Fallen Dragon*, the Greg Mandel novels: *Mindstar Rising*, *A Quantum Murder*, and *The Nano Flower*; *A Second Chance at Eden* (a collection of short stories set in the universe of *The Reality Dysfunction*) and the epic Night's Dawn trilogy, which includes *The Reality Dysfunction*, *The Neutronium Alchemist*, and *The Naked God*. Hamilton is working on his next novel.

FUTURES
(0446-61-062-3)

This stunning collection brings together a quartet of novellas by four of the most important voices in modern science fiction. From nanotech microcosms to infinite space, these brilliantly realized visions of worlds to come transcend the scope of imagination . . .

"Watching Trees Grow" by PETER F. HAMILTON
In an era of immortality and radical transition, murder is the ultimate crime—with no statute of limitations. And a relentless detective can pursue his quarry for centuries . . .

"Reality Dust" by STEPHEN BAXTER
A young man vows to investigate war criminals from Earth's alien occupation—even after humanity's past has been erased and reality itself may no longer exist . . .

"Making History" by PAUL McAULEY
On a ravaged space colony a historian from the winning side of The Quiet War sets out to chronicle the official story. But will history record the most important battle?

"Tendeleo's Story" by IAN McDONALD
An alien technolife called Chaga overruns Africa and infects its people—and a preacher's young daughter is at the center of its interstellar transformation . . .

VISIT WARNER ASPECT ONLINE!

THE WARNER ASPECT HOMEPAGE
You'll find us at: www.twbookmark.com then by clicking on Science Fiction and Fantasy.

NEW AND UPCOMING TITLES
Each month we feature our new titles and reader favorites.

AUTHOR INFO
Author bios, bibliographies and links to personal websites.

CONTESTS AND OTHER FUN STUFF
Advance galley giveaways, autographed copies, and more.

THE ASPECT BUZZ
What's new, hot and upcoming from Warner Aspect: awards news, bestsellers, movie tie-in information . . .